Here's what critics are saying about Catherine Brun's books:

"I highly recommend this series, and this book is one of the best!"
—*Kings River Life Magazine*

"Readers are sure to enjoy this playful tale...this book is bound to please anyone that is looking for an easy, satisfying read on the beach."
—*InD'tale Magazine*

"If you like your cozy mysteries complete with a cast of zany characters this is one for you. And guess what? Recipes are included which makes me really wish I could bake."
—*Night Owl Reviews*

"TASTES LIKE MURDER is an intriguing start to the *Cookies and Chance Mystery* series. I want to visit more with all of the quirky characters just to see what crazy and outrageous things they will do next!"
—*Fresh Fiction*

"Twistier than expected cozy read—great for beach or by the fire"
—*The Kindle Book Review*

BOOKS BY CATHERINE BRUNS

***Cookies & Chance Mysteries*:**
Tastes Like Murder
"A Spot of Murder" (novella)
Baked to Death
Burned to a Crisp
Frosted with Revenge
Silenced by Sugar
"Cookies, Chamomile, and Corpses" (novella)
Crumbled to Pieces
Sprinkled in Malice
Ginger Snapped to Death
Icing on the Casket
Knee Deep in Dough
Dessert is the Bomb
Seasoned with Murder
Bake, Batter & Roll

Aloha Lagoon Mysteries:
Death of the Big Kahuna
Death of the Kona Man

BAKE, BATTER, AND ROLL

a Cookies & Chance mystery

Catherine Bruns

Bake, Batter, and Roll

Design & background art by Janet Holmes using images under license from DepositPhotos.com.

Published by Gemma Halliday Publishing

BAKE, BATTER, AND ROLL

CHAPTER ONE

"What are you doing, Sal?" Josie Sullivan asked, as she stood behind me, watching as I peered out the window. "Shirking your cookie-making duties while you admire the view?"

I shielded my eyes from the sun and whirled to face her. "But it's such a great view, I can't help myself."

Sally's Samples, my bakery, was located directly across the street from where my new house had been built. As the owner of a one-man construction company, my husband Mike had completed about ninety percent of the work on the house by himself. It had taken longer than he'd planned, but was well worth the wait. We'd finally started moving our things in last week.

Mike was currently standing on the roof, shirtless, with the hot May sun beating down on him as he added rain gutters to the sides. At that moment, he happened to glance over at the bakery and spotted me at the window. He blew me a kiss.

"You guys are so in sync," Josie laughed.

I blew him a kiss back. "Yeah, we're always in something."

"Have you found a buyer for your other house yet?" She wanted to know.

"Not yet. We want to wait until everything's out before we start to schedule showings." I leaned my head against the window for a moment and closed my eyes, enjoying the feel of the sun on my face. Yes, I had everything I could want. The bakery was busy with customers—thanks in part to upcoming weddings and graduations. My new house was a dream come true, and I had a wonderful, loving family. It would be nice if I could slow down and enjoy it more, but there simply wasn't enough time.

"All right, stop sleeping on the job," Josie teased as she walked into the back room. "Want to help me make more fortune cookies? We're almost out. The sooner we finish, the sooner you can go pick up your little girl and get home to your man."

With one last wistful look in my husband's direction, I dutifully followed Josie into the kitchen and began to line cookie sheets with parchment paper. "There's no man for me to come home to tonight. After Mike gets done with the gutters, he has another job to rush off to and won't be done until about nine o'clock. He's spent so much time working on our house these past few months that he's neglected all his other jobs. You know, the paying ones. And we sort of need them, with all the bills coming in."

Josie set a large plastic container of flour on the table. She measured some out and then combined it in a bowl along with egg whites, vanilla, sugar, and cinnamon. I helped her spread the dough into thin circles and then whisked the pan into the oven. Making fortune cookies was a far different process than for regular cookies. We could only bake four to six at a time because the dough hardened quickly.

Sally's Samples sold thirty different varieties of cookies, with fortune cookies being our most popular. Customers receive a free one with every purchase. The messages inside had led to some strange incidents over the last few years, but I constantly told myself that they were merely a coincidence. For a while, I'd even entertained the ridiculous notion that my fortune cookies could predict the future.

Josie studied me as I spread dough on another cookie pan. "What are you staring at?" I asked.

She folded her arms across her chest. "Okay, level with me. What's going on? You haven't been yourself for the last couple of weeks."

"Everything's fine."

"Don't lie to me," she said. "I know you better than anyone—wait, I take that back. I know you better than anyone *except* for Mike and your grandmother. Hey, we've only been best friends for twenty-five years."

I smiled. "Twenty-five years this August."

Josie took the tray from me and placed it in the oven then removed a finished one and set it on the cooling rack. "Close enough. I came to your eighth birthday party. You invited everyone from our class. We sat next to each other while you blew out the candles and made a secret pledge to always be best friends."

"Hah!" I snorted. "You told me that we were going to be best friends whether I liked it or not. And I was too scared of you to argue."

Josie's hands flew as she placed a message inside the piece of cooked dough and quickly rolled up the sides around it. "Well, what can I say. I've always been a bit intimidating."

"It's been a great twenty-five years." My voice choked up with sudden emotion. "And I hope we have many more."

"All right, Sal, let's have it." Josie wiped her hands on her apron. "The truth. What the heck is wrong? You should be on top of the world. You've got a handsome husband who adores you, a sweet little girl, and a new house. Plus, you haven't found a dead body in months."

I couldn't argue with that. The last part was something most people didn't have to contend with. Ever since I'd returned to my hometown of Colwestern, New York five years ago, I'd seen more dead bodies than the local coroner. They had a way of turning up when I least expected them. Because of this, everyone in town thought of me as some kind of detective, which although flattering, couldn't be further from the truth.

I'd simply been in the wrong place at the wrong time. At least, that's what I always told myself.

"Maybe my luck has turned," I quipped and placed a strip of paper with the message, *You are worth a fortune*, on a piece of cooked dough. "The last time I found one was back in January, when we were on the cruise to the Bahamas." To be more precise, a dead body had fallen on me.

My eyes filled with tears, a common problem these days. "Let's talk about this another time, okay?"

"Sal, you're crying." Josie put an arm around my shoulders. "Please tell me what's wrong. Is your grandmother sick? Or your parents?"

I tried to blink away the tears. "No, everyone's fine. It's just pure happiness. I have everything I could possibly want out of life." This might be true, but I was also exhausted with taking care of Cookies, moving, and working at the bakery.

"What about Cookie? Is she okay?"

"Yes, she learned three new words this week," I said proudly. Don't mind me, I'm just tired."

"Where is the baby today? With your grandmother?"

Josie asked.

"Yes, Cookie's keeping her company while Mom and Dad are out of town." I honestly didn't know what my family would ever do without Grandma Rosa. Mike and I had named our baby daughter after her, but for now, we called her Cookie. It seemed appropriate. No one could ever have enough cookies in their life.

Grandma Rosa and Mike were my rocks, and I loved them both dearly. My grandmother had a rare quality that drew people to her. Besides being adored by everyone, she was also an excellent cook, seamstress, and crocheter. Grandma Rosa never judged anyone and always gave sound advice.

"I'm worried about you," Josie confessed.

I waved hand dismissively in the air. "It's nothing. I've been a little under the weather lately, that's all."

Josie's blue eyes widened, and she put a hand against her mouth. "Oh. My. God. Are you pregnant? I know how much you and Mike want another baby!"

"No." Disappointment settled in my chest. "I took a test yesterday, but it came out negative."

"That's too bad." Josie's expression was sympathetic. "But it will happen, Sal, and always when you least expect it. Remember when we were in high school? I always said I wasn't going to have any kids, but I wound up with four boys. If Rob hadn't had a vasectomy, I'd probably have ten by now."

Her comment made me chuckle because there was some truth to it. Everyone used to tease Josie that all her husband had to do was look at her, and bam! She was pregnant.

"You've been working too hard," Josie said. "The moving hasn't helped, either. Plus, you've got a toddler to run after. You need to slow down."

She was right, but there was nothing I could do about it. I couldn't shake the worrisome feeling that something was seriously wrong with me. It had broken my heart when the test came out negative. Our new house had four bedrooms, and I longed to fill them with siblings for Cookie.

I placed another message on a piece of dough and read it to myself while I worked. *Stardom is in your future*. Oh, brother. I began to roll the dough, but it had already hardened. "Shoot. I've done it again."

"No worries." Josie popped another tray into the oven.

"Listen, have you thought about asking Dodie to come in an extra day every week so you can have more time with Cookie?"

I spooned more batter onto the tray. "Wow. I never thought I'd hear you say that." Dodie Albert was our only part-time employee, except for a driver we used on special occasions. Dodie was a sweet lady in her sixties with a sunny disposition but could be accident prone at times Josie had little patience for the woman most days, but I gave her credit for trying.

Josie's mouth twisted into a smile. "What can I say? I'm mellowing in my old age."

The silver bells jingled on the front door, announcing that we had a customer. Josie whisked another tray of cookies into the oven and held up a hand. "I'll grab it, Sal."

I finished spooning out the dough, and placed the tray in the oven while Josie went into the storefront. While I tidied up the prep area, she came rushing back into the kitchen, her face as red as her hair. "You'd better get out there, Sal. You're not going to believe this."

Good grief. What now? There was never a dull moment in my life. With a sigh, I dried my hands and followed Josie into the storefront. Two men were positioning a camera on a tripod while a third man stood nearby, watching them. He turned in our direction and smiled. He was about forty, with thick sideburns and long dark hair pulled back in a ponytail.

"Yes, hello! Are you Sally Donovan?" he asked.

"I am. Um, what's going on here?"

He extended a hand. "Allow me to introduce myself. Corey Whitaker, director of *Senior Moments*."

What the heck was he talking about? Sure, I had senior moments, but I didn't go around advertising them. "It's—nice to meet you. What's the camera for?"

Josie looked like she might burst with excitement. "Sal, you've got to be kidding. *Senior Moments* is awesome. Don't tell me that you've never watched it."

I gave her a blank stare and shifted uncomfortably under Corey's intense gaze. "No, I'm afraid that I haven't."

"Senior Moments was created in the vein of the old game show, The Dating Game," Josie explained. "You remember that show, right? It was around in the seventies, and then they resurrected it in the nineties, I think. This is just a more current version."

"That still doesn't explain what these people are doing in my bakery," I said.

Corey laughed with delight and sidestepped my question. "Sorry that we're late. Don't worry, we'll get everything set up for tomorrow's show in a jiffy. As far as the actual taping goes, we should be able to wrap it up in one day if we start bright and early tomorrow. You realize that the bakery will need to be closed while filming is going on, correct?"

"What?" I shrieked. "I can't close the bakery. We'd lose too much money. And I never gave permission for this!"

A man in a light-blue polo shirt pushed through the front door and watched as two men erected a faux wall at the bottom of my staircase. He picked up one of the chairs from a nearby table and placed it on the other side of the wall.

"Hey Slim, come here for a second," Corey called.

Slim put down the chair and obediently came over to us. His name was appropriate, for he was well over six feet tall and as thin as a pencil, with short dark hair cut in a buzz cut. "What's up?" he asked.

"Do you think we'll need to put walls between the contestants?" Corey asked. "For most of the shows we use them, but I'm thinking maybe one this time to separate Earl from the ladies will be enough."

Slim placed his hands on his hips as his gaze roamed over the room. "Yeah, I think that'll work fine. The contestants can sit at individual tables out in the open."

Corey thought about this for a second then nodded in agreement. "I like it. And this way we can capture the dirty looks between the women as they duke it out over Earl."

"Who's Earl?" I asked.

Slim ignored me. "Here's my vision. Earl can stay upstairs in the vacant apartment until it's time to come down. We'll have the contestants wait in the kitchen area until he's situated, and then we'll seat them at their tables. Maybe with coffee and a cookie decorated with sprinkles—something colorful and happy."

A broad grin stretched across Corey's face. "Where have you been all my life? What a great eye for detail. The TV studio needs to employ you on a regular basis. Man, this is great."

It didn't sound so great to me. "Look, I never said that my bakery could be used for—"

"Our famous fortune cookies have sprinkles on them," Josie volunteered. "Customers get a free one with every purchase. Speaking of the cookies, I need to get the rest out of the oven. Be right back."

"Perfect!" Corey said as Josie hurried into the kitchen "It all fits. Picture this—three lonely and elderly women willing to do anything to go on a trip with the man of their dreams. Oh, Mrs. Donovan, allow me to introduce Slim Daniels. He's my right-hand man for this episode."

Slim nodded to me. "The pleasure's all mine. You've got a great little place here." He turned his attention to the cream-colored lace tablecloths my grandmother had crocheted for each table when the bakery first opened. "These add a nice touch. Classy. Yeah, I think we'll keep them for the taping."

"It does give the place more of a cozy feel," Corey agreed, as Josie returned. "One where you'd like to sit down with tea and crumpets and your new *Senior Moments* date."

"Maybe the couple could each open a fortune cookie after they're paired up," Josie said excitedly. "To further seal their fate."

Okay, this had gone too far. I waved my hand to get everyone's attention. "Sorry, but I never authorized a taping of this show. I'm afraid I'll have to ask you to leave."

Corey laughed. "No one ever says no to *Senior Moments*."

Just watch me. Seriously, who did this guy think he was?

Corey continued, oblivious to me. "One of our contestants nominated Sally's Samples for the shoot, and they even sent us pictures of your bakery. We've never done a taping in a bakery before, so this is perfect. Sure, I realize that closing a business for the day will result in lost sales, but no worries. You'll be generously compensated for your time and the use of the building. Now, if you can provide me with an email address, I'll email the contract over for your review and signature. Oh, and by the way, you don't even need to be here tomorrow. As long as we have a way to get into the building, we'll be all set."

"Um, I still don't know about this. What if someone gets hurt in my bakery while the taping's going on? I don't think—"

"All the details are in the contract," Corey interrupted. "If an accident occurs, the network's insurance will cover it. You can have an attorney look it over if you like."

"My younger sister is an attorney," I said. "She'll have to approve it before I say yes." Gianna worked as a criminal defense attorney with a local firm. I was certain she would go over it with a fine-toothed comb.

"No problem." Corey looked unconcerned as he turned back to Slim. "What about wardrobe? Did they get ahold of that local woman on the list?"

Josie's blue eyes shone with excitement. "Mr. Whitaker, I know you said it's not necessary for us to be here, but I'd like to watch, if that's okay."

"Of course!" Corey looked pleased. "Hey, it's your bakery. We just can't have any customers in here during the taping."

"Who did you say nominated us?" Corey and his crew were making me feel like an intruder in my own bakery. "Um, I'm still not sure that this is a good idea—"

"Excuse us for a second." Josie shot Corey a winning smile, then grabbed my arm and dragged me into the back room. She closed the door behind us and faced me. "Sal, do you realize what you're doing? This is the chance of a lifetime! Smiley Jones himself will be in your bakery! How many people can say that?"

Had she gone bananas? "I don't even know who Smiley Jones is. I'm more concerned about my bakery's reputation." My concern was valid. Over the years, the bakery had been associated with several murders. There were times when I felt like Sally's Samples reputation—and mine—were literally hanging from an apron string. "I don't care about the money or who Smiley Jones is."

Josie shook her head in disbelief. "You must be the only person alive who has never seen *Senior Moments* or heard of Smiley. Besides *The Bachelor*, it's the most popular dating show in the world. Get with the times, girlfriend. Everyone is fascinated with geriatric dating!"

Everyone except me. "Sorry, I guess I've been asleep for too long."

She shot me a dubious look. "Listen, Rip Van Winkle. Do you know how much business this taping might drive our way? It will do wonders for the bakery. Double, or maybe even *triple*, our sales! Millions of people watch *Senior Moments* every week."

"Look, I couldn't care less if…" Josie's words finally sank in. "Did you say millions?"

"Millions." Josie beamed. "It's hugely popular. Plus, the host, Smiley Jones, always makes it a point to thank the business owner during the episode. If there's time, he even brings them on air! The show goes to different locations for every taping, which is part of its unique charm. Their motto is, 'Spread senior love all around the world.'"

Good grief. "Okay, then, please enlighten me as to how our baked goods can help seniors find love."

"There's three contestants, plus the eligible bachelor or bachelorette," Josie explained. "The bachelor doesn't see the contestants during the show, and vice versa. He asks them personal questions about themselves, they answer, and then he decides who he wants to take with him on vacation."

I tried not to wince. "These questions—are they about delicate matters?"

"Nothing X-rated," Josie assured me. "But some of the contestants can be a bit graphic. I swear, their mouths have no filter."

I wasn't sure that I was ready for this. "And they go on vacation together—*alone*? After only knowing each other for an hour?"

Josie laughed out loud. "Sal, you are so old-fashioned. Take it to the next level! People have been doing this kind of thing for years. The only difference is that these contestants are older."

Unlike Josie, I was not a fan of reality TV. I rarely watched any television, especially with Cookie to keep me busy at all hours. Josie's kids were older, and she liked nothing better than to unwind with her shows after the kids were in bed. "The whole thing sounds a bit weird to me." I tried to picture my grandmother on such a kooky show and failed miserably. The entire concept was insane.

How desperate were people to answer intimate questions on TV for a vacation with someone they didn't even know? "It sounds crazy."

As we talked, Josie and I began to remove the fortune cookies from the baking rack and placed them on a tray for the display case. "Even the younger generation watches *Senior Moments*," she went on. "The only thing crazy is wanting to pass up such an amazing opportunity. When will we get another chance to have the bakery on TV!"

Josie must have amnesia. We'd once been contestants on *Cookie Crusades*, a popular baking show from the Food Network where we'd been pitted against other bakeries ready to kill for a chance at the monetary grand prize. Another time we had been invited to appear on *Someone's in the Kitchen with Donna,* a cooking and talk show reminiscent of Rachael Ray's. Both shows had been canceled shortly after our episodes had aired. Coincidence? I didn't think so.

"We're simply loaning them the use of the bakery for one day." Josie's voice turned pleading. "Less than twenty-four hours. Come on, Sal. I'll stay here the entire time to make sure nothing goes wrong. You can spend the day catching up on your sleep or with Cookie. Take advantage of the time. You need a break. It's obvious how exhausted you are."

"All right." I finally gave in. The taping meant a great deal to Josie, and the idea of increasing our volume excited me. "But is this how they always operate? Pick a location at random and waltz right in?"

"He said that one of our customers nominated the bakery." Josie's hand flew to her mouth. "Oh, Lord. Do you think it was your father? Maybe he wants to be a contestant."

"Oh, please. Dad on a dating show? My mother would have something to say about that." My parents liked a challenge and were always ready for new adventures, but I couldn't picture this. Dad would try anything once, but a dating show wasn't his cup of tea.

Josie shrugged. "Hey, it was only a suggestion. You never know with him. Are they back from their trip yet?"

"Not until tomorrow. They fly into New York City from Bermuda this evening and will spend the night there. Tomorrow morning, they'll take a flight home from JFK. Gianna's picking them up at the airport."

"They're on their second honeymoon, right?" Josie grinned. "But I'm not sure that they ever finished their first one."

My parents were still as deeply in love as they had been on their wedding day, thirty-five years ago. If there were ever two people perfectly suited for each other, it was them. "I'm glad they were able to get away. This was their first vacation alone since Dad bought the funeral home."

Josie opened the door. "Come on. Let's get back out there before Corey decides to find another location."

Corey looked like he had no intention of leaving. He was chatting with his two crew members about moving the tables farther apart. "Yeah, that looks about right. And no partitions, guys. We want the women to see each other the entire time." He turned to me. "Well, what did you decide?"

"All right," I sighed. "As long as the contract is okay with my sister, the taping can take place tomorrow. But it has to be wrapped up in one day."

"Excellent." Corey rubbed his hands together in satisfaction. "Expect us here at seven o'clock on the dot."

"I'll be waiting," Josie assured him.

"One more thing," I said. "Who recommended my bakery for *Senior Moments*?"

Corey shuffled through some papers on his clipboard. "Let's see. I've got the name in here somewhere."

The silver bells on the front door jingled, announcing we had a customer. My grandmother and Mrs. Gavelli were standing by the entrance. There couldn't be two women more different from each other. While my grandmother was adored by all, Nicoletta Gavelli was the proverbial thorn in everyone's rosebush. She had lived next door to my parents for over thirty years and never had a nice thing to say about anyone, especially me.

Mrs. Gavelli had caught me playing doctor with her grandson in our garage when I was only six years old. It didn't matter that Johnny had initiated the game—she'd always blamed me instead. Johnny was now married to Gianna, and they had a son—my nephew, Alex. He was nine months older than Cookie.

Always happy to see my grandmother, I kissed her on the cheek. She represented the normalcy that my bakery needed right now. "We're kind of in the middle of something," I said.

"If you're here for Nicoletta's weekly fortune cookie haul, Sal can bring them home tonight," Josie offered.

Mrs. Gavelli gave a loud harrumph and glowered at us. She was dressed in her usual outfit of black, which included housecoat, stockings, and Birkenstocks. It didn't matter if it was ten below zero or ninety degrees outside, she always dressed the same. "You not telling us anything we don't know, missy," she said. "I first one to know about TV show."

Josie glared back at her. "Come off it, old woman. Why would you be the first one to know?"

Mrs. Gavelli stabbed herself in the chest with a bony

finger. "Because *I* am contestant, that why. And *I* gonna win."

CHAPTER TWO

I should have seen the writing on the wall. Apparently, it was too much to ask that a normal customer had recommended my bakery. Mrs. Gavelli always did exactly as she pleased without bothering to consult anyone.

"You're such a troublemaker," Josie spat out. "You should have told Sal."

"It would have been nice if I'd had some notice." I turned to my grandmother. "Why didn't you say anything?"

Grandma Rosa rolled her eyes at the ceiling, something she rarely did. "Because I did not know, *cara mia.* Nicoletta never breathed a word about it to me until a few minutes ago. I thought we were only coming here to get her weekly supply of fortune cookies."

Mrs. Gavelli wasn't fond of me, but she adored my fortune cookies. She thought of them as her personal horoscope and had gotten into the habit of opening one every morning.

"Hah. You see?" She stared at my grandmother in triumph. "Your granddaughter—she think you know all, Rosa. But no—you don't."

My grandmother snorted. "Nicoletta, you are—what do they say? A loony song."

I tried to hide my smile. "I think you mean loony tune, Grandma."

"That is good too," she agreed.

Mrs. Gavelli pushed past us and marched over to Corey. He was in the middle of a conversation with Slim. When he looked up and noticed her, his jaw dropped. "What the heck—I mean, *who* are you?"

Mrs. Gavelli proudly lifted her nose in the air. "I be Nicoletta Gavelli. And I not come here to lose."

Slim checked his clipboard. "She's one of the

contestants."

"Yikes," Corey muttered. "What's this world coming to? All right, what do you want, hon?"

Mrs. Gavelli shoved a finger in his face. "You no honey me, little boy. You show respect for elders."

Corey blinked once—no, twice, and started to say something, but Slim placed a hand on his shoulder and quickly spoke up. "Ma'am, if you plan to be on the show tomorrow morning, you'll need to wear something more colorful."

Mrs. Gavelli stared down at her outfit. "What da matter with this?" she asked. "Black, she be my signature color."

"You look like the Grim Reaper," Josie blurted out.

"Never mind, Slim," Corey said. "I kind of like it that she's an oddball. The public will eat it up." He turned back to Mrs. Gavelli. "Make sure that you're here by seven o'clock tomorrow morning, understand? The other two contestants will be here as well, and all three of you need to be in makeup and wardrobe by eight, before we start taping."

She let out a loud sniff. "I be here. But no need for other contestants. I gonna win."

"Yeah, sure. Whatever." Corey's mouth crinkled at the corners. "You're a unique one, that's for sure. I have a feeling this is all gonna work out well."

As he and Slim walked up the stairs to my vacant apartment deep in discussion, I had my doubts. Whenever Mrs. Gavelli was involved, nothing went well.

She shot me a smug smile. "You see? They not mess with Nicoletta Gavelli."

"What about Ronald?" Josie wanted to know. "Isn't he upset that you're looking for love in all the wrong places?"

Ronald Feathers was Mrs. Gavelli's eighty-something-year-old boyfriend. He took the verbal abuse that she heaped on him with a grain of salt, but he was no angel, either. Ronald had three ex-wives and would be paying alimony to all of them until he reached the pearly gates himself. Ronald's most notable feature was that he had more hair in his ears than on his head. He was also hard of hearing, but that wasn't a bad thing where Mrs. Gavelli was concerned.

Mrs. Gavelli sniffed. "Ronald and me, we have understanding. If I go on trip with some man, it strictly platonic. No hanky panky. And Ronald, he stay home and watch my house.

He gotta watch his pennies anyway."

"That's right," Josie said. "His ex-wives have made sure pennies are all he has left." She grabbed my arm in excitement. "This is going to be so much fun. Now, all we have to do is sit back and watch the money roll in. What could possibly go wrong?"

Famous last words. With Mrs. Gavelli involved? Only everything.

* * *

Because I had an eighteen-month-old baby in the house, I no longer needed an alarm clock to wake me in the morning. Cookie's lungs began working at five o'clock sharp. I would dress her and feed her while Mike showered, and then he would watch her as I got ready for work. After Mike left, Cookie and I would bond over more breakfast—mine this time—pack up the car, and I would drop her off at the designated babysitter's house for the day. I still brought her to the bakery with me once in a while, but now that she was getting older, she was a handful and into everything.

The next morning, my subconscious state must have realized that I didn't need to be at the bakery, because I slept way past five o'clock. I vaguely remembered Mike telling me to stay in bed and he would take care of Cookie. When they left, she'd kissed my face repeatedly until it tickled and shouted, "Bye, Ma!" in my ear. Mike had arranged his schedule so that I could have the entire day to myself. As much as I wanted to be with my daughter, I needed sleep to function.

An insistent buzzing interrupted the current dream I was having. I tried to ignore it, but the sound kept repeating in my head. With a groan, I opened my eyes to see what it was. That was when I noticed the screen of my cellphone was lit up on the nightstand. As I reached for the phone, it stopped ringing. With a grunt, I dropped the phone and snuggled back under the covers. A second later, the phone buzzed again, and I snatched it up. "Hello?"

"Where the heck are you?" Josie asked.

Blinking sleep out of my eyes, I glanced at the time. Nine fifteen. Holy cow. I'd been in slumberland for over eleven hours! With a start, I jumped out of bed, searching for clothes. "Oh my

God! I'm so sorry, Jos. Is it really busy? I'll be there in fifteen minutes. I just need to feed the baby first." I stopped and listened, half expecting to hear her cry, but only silence met my ears. "Cookie must have taken the car."

"What are you saying?" Josie laughed. "You're still half asleep. Look, I'm sorry that I woke you. The bakery is closed today, remember? But you do need to come in at some point this morning. Corey has another paper for you to sign. I guess the TV studio forgot to email it yesterday, but he's got a copy here. I'd sign for you, but it must be signed by the owner."

"Okay, sure." I yawned and stretched and then ran into the bathroom. I began to brush my teeth with the phone pressed against my ear. "How's everything going? Did they start taping yet?"

An awkward silence came from the other end. "Um, not yet. There's been a little problem."

The word problem was synonymous with Mrs. Gavelli. "Okay, what did she do this time?"

"Nothing for you to worry about." Josie tried to sound cheerful. "The place is still standing. Just get here as soon as you can."

I showered, dressed, and thirty minutes later, hurried out the door with a mug of coffee in hand. When I arrived at the bakery three minutes later, a huge crowd of people was standing by the front door, trying to peek inside. It was obvious that news of the taping had leaked out, but how?

At that moment, I spotted a television production truck and a white paneled van parked at the curb. A giant sign in my front window with bold black lettering read, *Closed due to Senior Moments taping.*

Jeez, what a relief that they were being discreet about it.

As I rounded a corner to park my car behind the bakery, someone stepped into the direct path of my car. Panicked, I slammed on the brakes. When I glanced out the window and saw who it was, I almost wished that I had run him down instead.

"Sally Donovan!" Jerry Maroon waved a microphone against my half-open window. "Tell us all about the taping of *Senior Moments* happening today. Inquiring minds need to know! One of your blinds is broken, and I saw Smiley Jones inside. How about you introduce me?"

Disgusted, I raised the window, almost pinching Jerry's

hand in the process, and pressed my gas pedal all the way to the floor. Jerry was a migraine waiting to happen. He had started out as an anchorman on Channel Eleven, been fired for sexual harassment, and then turned to a career as columnist for the *Colwestern Journal*. Afterward, he'd joined Channel Nine and, to the best of my knowledge, was still working both jobs. He enjoyed making my bakery the butt of his jokes by referring to it as Sally's Shambles.

Because of Jerry's relentlessness, he'd almost been the victim of a psychopathic killer last year, with me going along for the ride. After Jerry had stared death in the face, he'd promised to become a kinder, gentler soul.

What a joke.

There were three parking spots situated in the alley behind my bakery. One was occupied by Josie's minivan and another by an unknown sedan, which I assumed belonged to someone from the show. I hurried out of my car and towards the door before Jerry had a chance to waylay me again. As I reached for the knob, the door flew open. Josie grabbed me by the arm and yanked me inside, slamming the door behind us.

"What the heck is going on?" I demanded.

She threw up her hands. "That old woman is about to ruin everything. I'm surprised they've put up with her for this long."

I sucked in some air. "What did Mrs. Gavelli do?"

"She chased off the other female contestants," Josie explained. "They were getting ready to start taping, with each woman sitting at her designated table. Mrs. Gavelli walked over and said something to each woman and then, the next thing we all knew, they were running for the door as fast as they could."

Cripes. I slumped against the wall. "I'm so sorry you had to deal with all of this. Do they have to cancel the taping?"

Josie paused with her hand on the door. "It's not your fault, Sal. I was the one who wanted to watch the taping. And I'm not sure what they're planning to do. Corey's had his staff on the phone with alternate contestants for the last half hour. If they don't come up with a plan soon, they may have to, or at the very least, postpone it."

I followed Josie into the storefront. The partition was in place at the foot of the stairs, with the phrase, *Have you had your Senior Moment today?* plastered on it. A couple of crew members were standing at one side of the room, chatting on their cells. The rest were involved in a deep discussion. Corey and Slim were standing by themselves on the opposite side, talking in earnest. Neither one of them looked happy.

"It's not going to work," Slim insisted. "Why don't you forget about it? There must be another location you could use for tomorrow."

"No, it has to be done today," Corey replied.

Mrs. Gavelli was sitting at the middle table, arms folded across her chest. The wardrobe department must have worked their magic, because she wore a yellow polka dotted scarf wrapped around her white hair. The rest of her outfit was the same as always.

She shook her fist at Slim. "You no gonna forget nothing. I sign contract. We tape show now. End of discussion."

Corey shot Mrs. Gavelli a look that suggested he'd like to see her six feet under. "For God's sake, woman, don't you understand? We can't tape the show with only one contestant. You chased the other ones away! And don't you ever listen? We told you to wear something with color."

Yikes. Corey had become a different person overnight and needed an attitude adjustment. It was understandable, though. Mrs. Gavelli would have tried Mother Theresa's patience if she'd had the chance.

"She never listens to anyone," Josie remarked.

"Black, she good color for me." Mrs. Gavelli tapped her forehead. "That chunky girl make me wear this. I got color now."

Corey pinched his nose between his thumb and forefinger. "I need to start drinking heavily."

A crew member came over and whispered something in Slim's ear.

"No worries, Cor," Slim said. "It's going to work. The other woman said yes. We only need to find one more contestant."

"You can't be serious." Corey looked stunned. "You want me to take a recommendation from *her*?"

Slim lowered his voice, but I could still hear him. "We don't have any choice if you want the taping done today. Let's just suck it up and get this job done. I can go out on the street and grab the first woman over sixty-five that I see. Who cares what she looks like." He pointed at Mrs. Gavelli. "She couldn't be any worse than this one!"

Before Corey could reply, an earthshattering crash sounded from the kitchen. Josie cursed while I shut my eyes in frustration.

"What was that?" Corey asked.

"Sounds like my employee," I sighed.

Dodie Albert appeared in the doorway and gave a little wave. She stared over at Josie and me, her face as red as a tomato. "Hello, girls."

"Dodie, what are you doing here?" I asked. "I told you we're not open for business today."

The elderly woman looked sheepish. "I know, Sally, but I left my phone in the kitchen yesterday. And now, when I went to reach for it, I had a little accident."

"What else is new." Josie ran into the kitchen.

This kind of thing happened all the time with Dodie. I'd hired her on a part-time basis when Cookie was born, needing more flexibility in my schedule. She was an excellent baker and the customers loved her, but it was rare that we got through a day without her dropping a dozen eggs or a tray of fortune cookies. Nevertheless, her heart was in the right place, and I couldn't bring myself to fire her.

Dodie tried to retreat to the kitchen, but Corey stopped her. "Hold on. You work here?"

"She no work," Mrs. Gavelli yelled. "That woman walking disaster."

"Yes, indeed." A brilliant grin crossed Dodie's face. "I'm Dodie."

Josie reappeared from the kitchen. "Only some dented trays this time," she muttered to me. "Maybe she's finally improving."

Corey studied Dodie like she was a bug under a microscope. He grinned and extended his hand. "Hi, Dodie. I'm Corey Whitaker, director of *Senior Moments*."

She gasped. "Oh, wow, I love that show."

"How would you like to be on television today?" he asked.

Mrs. Gavelli frowned. "Her? You gonna put clumsy on show?"

"I would love it!" Dodie's face lit up like a Christmas tree. "Of course, I've always wanted to guest star on a soap opera. Those are my favorite. But there aren't as many of them around anymore. Not like when I was growing up. Why, when I was in high school, I would rush home from school to watch *Guiding Light*, *Another World*, and—"

Corey cast an appealing glance at Slim, who sighed heavily. He dutifully took Dodie by the elbow. "Come with me, ma'am," he said. "We'll need some signatures, and then our makeup artist, Tina, will get to work on you."

Mrs. Gavelli shot Dodie a death glare as she followed Slim upstairs. "She better not cost me trip," she spat out. "I be the one going to Italy."

"Italy?" I asked in surprise. "That's the grand prize?"

Corey nodded. "Yes, it's an all-expense paid trip for two. Five nights in Rome, and five nights in Sicily. *Senior Moments* has even included first-class plane tickets."

Josie's eyes widened. "Wow. That must have cost a fortune. I'm tempted to run out and buy myself a silver-haired wig."

"Don't you dare," I laughed.

Corey gratefully accepted the cup of coffee that a crew member had run out and bought for him. He took a long sip. "Thanks, Pete. Well, it looks like we're ready to roll. Earl's finished with wardrobe, and now that we have Dodie, everything is all set."

"Earl's the eligible bachelor they'll be fighting over." Josie snorted. "You should see the guy. He looks like death warmed over."

I shook my head. "Real nice, Jos."

Corey almost smiled. "Mrs. Donovan, she's actually being kind."

Good grief. If *Senior Moments* did have high ratings, this week's episode was sure to bring them down. With ancient Earl as the eligible bachelor and snarky Mrs. Gavelli plus naïve Dodie as contestants, why the heck would anyone want to watch?

Then again, what did I care? I was getting paid for the use of my bakery. Once the show aired, I'd surely start to see an increase in business. This wasn't personal for me. Sure, Dodie was an employee, but not a member of my family. And Mrs. Gavelli was related to my sister, not me. Thank goodness for small favors.

"Wait a minute." I held up a finger as the silver bells jingled on the front door. "That's only two contestants—Mrs.

Gavelli and Dodie. Who's the third eligible bachelorette?"

"That would be me," Grandma Rosa called out.

CHAPTER THREE

"No way," I whispered. "You can't be serious."

Grandma Rosa's face was taut and the color of powdered sugar. "I am afraid it is true, *cara mia*."

"Stop it." Josie put a hand over her mouth.

This couldn't be happening. My grandmother was too sensible and dignified to appear on a television dating show. She even once told me how much she loathed them. Heck, Grandma didn't even watch television. The whole thing was absurd, and the thought of her dating was unconceivable. Simply out of the question. Grandma Rosa hadn't been involved with another man since my grandfather had died thirty years ago.

I was only three years old when my grandfather passed away, and as a result, I remembered nothing about him. It wasn't until many years later that Grandma Rosa had taken me into her confidence. Much to my surprise, she'd confided to me that Grandpa had not been her one true love. The honor belonged to a man she had met in Italy as a teenager. His name was Vernon and he had been a soldier visiting Italy at the time. Like Romeo and Juliet, their love story had ended far too soon.

My great-grandfather had disapproved of the relationship and forbade Grandma Rosa to ever see him again. Soon afterwards, Vernon had gone away to serve in the Vietnam War. They'd been able to correspond for a while, but then Vernon's letters had stopped suddenly. A few years later, Grandma Rosa left Italy after she married my grandfather. They'd settled in New York, where my mother was born. She never heard from Vernon again.

Grandma Rosa raised her eyebrows at me. "This was not my choice, *cara mia.* After Nicoletta scared off the other two contestants, she called and demanded that I come down here. I am only doing this so the crazy old woman will not make more trouble for anyone."

"Who you call crazy?" Mrs. Gavelli wanted to know.

"Pinch me. I still don't believe it," Josie said. "But what happens if you win?"

My grandmother threw up her hands. "I do not know. I do not want to know. There is no way that I will go to Italy with a strange man. All I can do is hope for the best and just go with the show."

I had to think about that one for a minute. "It's flow. You're going with the flow."

"Whatever." Grandma Rosa shrugged. "Stop correcting me, *cara mia*. I have a headache."

Josie and I exchanged a horrified glance. My grandmother never spoke to me in that manner. I had been correcting her mixed-up sayings for years, and she always took it with a grain of salt.

The makeup artist, a pretty blonde named Tina, hurried down the stairs and motioned at my grandmother. "Excuse me, hon, but we've got to hurry. Come on upstairs with me."

Corey was standing at the foot of the stairs. "Slim!" he yelled. "Is Smiley ready?"

"Both Smiley and Earl are good to go," Slim called back down. "We'll wait until the last contestant is seated then Earl will come on down."

After five minutes, Grandma Rosa reappeared, looking no different, except for some extra rouge on her cheeks. She was still wearing the same black slacks and beige cardigan as before. Once she was seated at a table next to Mrs. Gavelli and Dodie, footsteps sounded on the stairs followed by a rustling behind the partition. I was curious to get a look at Earl, but it would have to wait.

My watch read eleven thirty. Almost lunchtime. Taping was supposed to have started at seven o'clock, and I couldn't help but wonder how much longer these people would be in my bakery.

A man dressed in a gray pinstriped suit appeared from behind the partition. He went to stand by the podium that had *Senior Moments* written on it. Grandma Rosa was at a table with a number three on it, Mrs. Gavelli's had a two, and Dodie's a one. Tina went around to each of them doing last minute touchups.

"There you go, sweetie," she cooed at Dodie. "You're not

as shiny now."

Dodie wore a flowered blue and white blouse that I'd never seen before. Both she and Grandma Rosa looked like model contestants, while Mrs. Gavelli, clad in black, resembled Satan's twin.

"She looks more morbid than usual," Josie said, reading my mind.

Corey must have overheard, because he wagged a finger at a heavyset woman standing on the opposite side of the room, who immediately hurried over. The woman had long, stringy dark hair and skin so white that she resembled an albino. "It's Skye, right?" Corey asked.

"Yes, sir."

"Can't you do something with her outfit?"

Skye shook her head. "She refused to change, Mr. Whitaker. And I don't want to die young."

"We put you in charge of wardrobe today for a reason," he told her curtly. "It's your job to make these contestants look good. Don't expect us to hire you again if you can't follow orders."

The woman's dark eyes widened in amazement. She opened her mouth to say something then thought better of it. "Yes, sir."

Corey's tone sounded a bit harsh to me, but it wasn't my place to interfere.

The man in the gray suit gave Skye a onceover as she walked by him. He addressed Corey. "Where'd you get her from?"

"She's only here for the day," Corey said. "Hillary had a conflict, so I'm stuck with temps to help out. She's not exactly the pick of the litter, huh?"

Josie stared in awe at the man wearing the gray suit and nudged me. "That's Smiley."

Smiley was tall and slender, with dark hair slicked behind his ears. He caught my eye and waved gaily at Josie and me. It was easy to see how the man got his name. His lips curled into a wide grin, displaying a perfect set of teeth that were so bright they almost blinded me.

"He's the only one in the room who's smiling," I noted.

"It won't last," Josie observed. "Once he meets Nicoletta, it will disappear."

Slim, who'd overheard us, let out a snicker. "If you made his kind of money, you'd smile too."

"Okay, let's do this, people!" Corey shouted. "I'd like to be home before midnight. Is everyone ready? Here we go. *Senior Moments*, Episode 113. And…action!"

Carly Rae Jepsen's "Call Me Maybe" filtered through speakers, followed by a man's rumbling deep voice. "It's time to have a…Senior Moment! And here's the star of your show, Smiley Jones!"

Applause roared through the room. Things had changed drastically since Josie and I had appeared on *Cookie Crusades*. "No live studio audience, and music pumped through the speakers? Gosh, I feel old."

Josie's blue eyes twinkled at me. "Sorry, Sal, but you've got another thirty years before you can have a turn on this show."

"Gee, I can hardly wait," I said.

Slim held a finger to his lips, and we fell silent.

"Hi everyone, and thanks for joining us today on *Senior Moments*!" Smiley grinned and waved at a make-believe audience. He stood directly in front of Mrs. Gavelli's table, and I had to wonder if he was blocking her from the camera on purpose. "Who needs *The Bachelor* when you've got a show that's for mature adults only?"

"If it's so mature, why is Mrs. Gavelli here?" Josie whispered.

Smiley spread his arms out wide. "Folks, we have three lovely new contestants this week, who all hail from Colwestern, New York. Many of you might know that I grew up in Buffalo, so the entire area is near and dear to my heart. Each of these ladies would love to have a special senior moment with our handsome and eligible bachelor, Earl!"

Applause rang out as the camera moved from table to table. Grandma Rosa's expression was serious, Mrs. Gavelli shook her fist, and Dodie resembled a frozen statue.

Mrs. Gavelli kept peeking around Smiley, who tried to pretend she wasn't there. "Our location for this week's show is a Colwestern bakery called Sally's Samples, which is owned by Mrs. Sally Donovan. It's a pretty special place, folks. Mrs. Donovan has a unique talent that I've never seen before!"

"Unique talent. He means the fortune cookies, right?" I whispered.

Josie shrugged. "Maybe he's talking about the dead bodies you've found over the years. I don't know of any other baker who's got that going for them."

Smiley proudly displayed a fortune cookie in his hand. "Sally's Samples is a novelty cookie shop with many delicious varieties, but it's the fortune cookies that keep everyone coming back. And something tells me that the one in my hand holds the answer to who Earl will choose as his companion on a fabulous, all-expense-paid trip to Italy!"

"That be me!" Mrs. Gavelli shouted excitedly and jumped to her feet. She pushed Smiley out of the way with such force that he almost toppled over.

"Cut!" Corey yelled.

Slim nudged Corey. "Remember what you were saying? Maybe you should leave it in. The woman's a lunatic for sure, but hey, she's got spunk. Home viewers will love it."

"All right, fine. Whatever," Corey grumbled. "Anything to get us out of here sooner."

"Me," Mrs. Gavelli repeated as she stabbed herself in the chest. "He gonna pick me."

Corey narrowed his eyes at her. "No speaking until you're asked a direct question. And no shoving Smiley again. Got it? You can easily be replaced."

Mrs. Gavelli shot him a disbelieving look. "Nah. No one even come close."

Truer words were never spoken.

Corey cleared his throat. "Okay, let's try it again, folks. Smiley, raise the cookie in the air. Ready? Action!"

Smiley displayed his wide grin as he held up the fortune cookie.

"Jeez," Josie muttered. "I should have brought my sunglasses."

"Now, all of you at home can see Earl sitting in his private area, waiting for love," Smiley cooed.

A chorus of "Aww" came through the speakers.

Smiley continued. "But—our lovely contestants have not yet seen the eligible bachelor. Let's find out a little more about this particular stud."

"Did he say stud or dud?" Josie asked.

"He's head cashier at the local Jolly Green Grocer and an all-around great guy," Smiley read from an index card. "He's never been married and loves to collect old TV guides. Still a playboy in every right at the young age of seventy-nine, meet Earl Jacobsen!"

A roar of applause echoed through the room.

"I gotta see this guy," Mrs. Gavelli muttered and rose from the table.

"You!" Corey pointed at her. "Sit down. I'm warning you!" He waved at Smiley. "Go on, we're still rolling."

"Why no live audience?" I asked Slim, who was standing next to me.

He stared at me like I had two heads. "Please. This is only my first time working on this gig, but hardly any of them have live audiences anymore. Besides, can you imagine the Grim Reaper interacting with a live audience?"

It was a frightening thought, indeed.

"Now here comes the fun part," Josie said excitedly. "Smiley's going to ask the women all sorts of personal questions."

I felt a stab of pity for my grandmother. She was only doing this to appease Nicoletta. Grandma Rosa was a very private person. She didn't believe in airing one's dirty laundry, especially on national television. And while Nicoletta was a royal pain in the behind, I almost felt sorry for her as well. She was so bad tempered and snarky that there was no way Earl would ever choose her. It looked like Dodie would be the one going to Italy with the so-called eligible bachelor.

Smiley moved back behind the podium, looking grateful to be out of Nicoletta's reach. "Earl, it's all up to you now. Start asking questions and find your travel and soulmate!"

Yikes.

Josie drew up a chair and sat down. "I should have made popcorn."

Earl's nasally voice sounded from behind the partition. "Bachelorette number two. If we had a romantic evening at home, what would you be wearing?"

A loud *Ooooh,* vibrated through the speakers.

Mrs. Gavelli gave an exaggerated snicker. "I wear black."

Earl tried to make his voice sound seductive but failed miserably. He began coaghing like he might hack up a lung. "That sounds super sexy. You mean like a black lace teddy?"

Mrs. Gavelli shook her head vehemently. "I no wear animal fur."

Everyone looked confused by her response, especially Corey, who smacked himself in the head. There was a long pause before Earl spoke again. "Okay, moving on. Bachelorette number three, what would *you* be wearing on our date?"

Grandma Rosa tossed her head in disdain. "That is a silly question. Clothes, of course."

"Aha. Playing hard to get, I see," Earl chuckled.

Corey pulled so hard on his ponytail that he must have been in intense pain. "Just shoot me now. I don't get paid enough for this."

"What about you, bachelorette number one?" Earl asked.

Dodie looked like a deer caught in headlights. The blood had drained from her face as she sat there unmoving, staring at the camera.

"What's wrong with her?" Slim asked.

"Classic stage fright," Josie murmured.

Mrs. Gavelli got up and marched over to Dodie's table. Without missing a beat she promptly whacked the woman in the side of the head with her pocketbook. Dodie teetered back and forth in the chair for a second but caught herself before she hit the floor.

"You gotta wake up!" Mrs. Gavelli yelled. "This no time for nap!"

"Cut!" Slim shouted.

Corey glared at him. "Hey, I'm the only one allowed to say that! Never mind. Keep it rolling, Gus. With any luck, we could turn this into a show like Jerry Springer's."

"Homina, homina, homina," Dodie mumbled.

"Oh yeah. Keep talking dirty to me, baby," Earl purred. "I love it."

"This is sick," I said to Josie. "My grandmother doesn't need to be subjected to this garbage."

"Bachelorette number three," Earl continued. "If I came over to your house for dinner, what would you feed me?"

My grandmother seemed to relax a bit with this question. After all, cooking was one of her many specialties. She lifted her chin and stared directly into the camera. "We will start with pasta fagioli and some antipasto. Then for the main course we will have braciole with linguini, and ricotta cheesecake for dessert."

"Honey, that sounds marvelous." Earl began to breathe heavily, like an obscene phone caller, before he burst into another fit of coughing. "But I want *you* to be dessert."

"Oh, for cripes sake," I muttered. "He's a dirty old man! I don't want my grandmother doing this!"

"Shh." Slim held a finger against his lips. "People love this part of the show."

"And what about you, bachelorette number two?" Earl wanted to know. "What would you give me to eat?"

Mrs. Gavelli folded her arms across her chest. "If I like you, I make my famous chicken cacciatore. If no, maybe I feed you rat poison."

An awkward silence followed.

"Well, you're quite the spitfire, my little muffin," Earl finally said. "What about you, bachelorette number one?"

Dodie licked her lips in nervous anticipation. "Oh, I guess we'd have takeout. I can be a little clumsy in the kitchen, especially when I'm nervous."

Earl emitted a deep, low chuckle. "What about the other rooms of the house, honey?"

Another *Oooh* sounded through the speakers. Poor Dodie's face turned a crimson color. She turned so quickly toward the speakers that she fell off her chair.

Corey slammed the clipboard onto the floor as Slim ran over to help Dodie up. "Cut!"

"Hey, watch it! We just had those floors refinished," I said.

Mrs. Gavelli shook her head in disgust and jabbed a finger in Dodie's direction. "That one. She gonna ruin everything. She stay in bed forever."

"I hate to agree with Nicoletta on anything, but she has a valid point," Josie murmured.

Earl went on to ask the women what their idea of a perfect date was. Mrs. Gavelli's comment had to be censored, Grandma Rosa insisted that she didn't date, and Dodie said she liked to go to the movies. It made sense to me. After all, there wasn't much that she could destroy in a movie theater. After about another two hours of taping and Corey screaming "Cut" until he was hoarse, we finally reached the decision-making time.

"*This* is the big moment." Smiley grinned like a Cheshire cat. As he looked around the room at all of us, the smile faded. A brief look of uneasiness crossed his gaze, but in another second it disappeared. It made me wonder if something was wrong with him. He was obviously not enjoying his job, and I wondered why.

"Earl, we're all dying to hear your decision," Smiley said. "Which of these lovely ladies do you want to take to Italy with you for a romantic holiday? Will it be—bachelorette number three?"

Grandma Rosa shook her head at the camera.

"Bachelorette number two?" Smiley prompted as Mrs. Gavelli stood on her chair and started flapping her arms like a chicken.

"Or…bachelorette number one?"

"I don't feel so good," Dodie groaned and promptly threw up all over the table.

A curse word popped out of Corey's mouth, followed by, "Cut!"

Tina and Skye both helped Dodie out of her chair and upstairs to the bathroom.

"Hey!" Mrs. Gavelli yelled rudely. "She better not get to see studly man."

Slim produced a spray bottle of Lysol and went over to clean the table himself. "Yep, I'm never doing this again," he mumbled.

I glanced at my watch. Five o'clock on the dot. Would this day ever end? A tapping could be heard at the back door, and Josie hurried into the kitchen to see who it was. A minute later, Mike appeared in the doorway, holding Cookie by the hand. Her big blue eyes, so like her father's, shone with happiness when she saw me. "Ma-ma!" she called.

"My two favorite people." I joined them in the kitchen and swept Cookie up into my arms for a giant hug.

"I was curious to see how the taping was going." Mike leaned over to kiss me then wrinkled his nose. "Did you get sick?"

"Not me," I said. "Dodie had a classic case of stage fright."

He suppressed a grin. "I picked Cookie up from Johnny's and texted you to see if you wanted to go out for dinner. You never answered."

"Sorry. I had my phone on silent because of the taping." I shifted Cookie to my right hip and reached into my jeans pocket. "Oh, wait. I must have left it out here. Where'd I put my purse?"

"See." Cookie gave a little giggle and handed me my

phone.

Mike's mouth fell open. "Where the heck did she get that from?"

"You have to watch her like a hawk," I reminded him. "Was she near my purse?"

He looked confused. "I put my phone on silent before we went into the storefront. I took my eyes off her for maybe five seconds."

"That's all it takes." I rubbed my nose against Cookie's. "You shouldn't touch Mommy's things, baby."

"Baby, baby," Cookie babbled.

"How about you guys grab some takeout, and I'll meet you at home?" I suggested. "I'm too tired to go out. It's been quite an eventful day here."

Josie chuckled. "Yeah, that's for sure."

Mike grinned. "I'll bet it has. Okay, Cookie and I will grab some food and meet you at home. Try not to be too long, sweetheart."

He lifted Cookie in his arms, who waved happily at me. "Bye. Ma!"

"Bye, bye, precious. See you at home."

Josie and I pushed through the door into the storefront as Corey was yelling "Action," for about the five hundredth time today. He looked like he had aged ten years in the past ten hours.

Smiley stared at him in bewilderment. "Okay, where shall we take it from?"

"For God's sake," Corey roared. "Earl, tell us who you've selected so we can be done with this nightmare before Christmas!"

Smiley's grin faded as he picked up his index cards.

Corey gestured at Slim. "I don't know what the heck is wrong with him lately. Smiley is out of it. And I need to quit this job before it gives me a stroke."

"Smiley's been like that a lot lately," Slim agreed.

Slim's comment had confused me. Didn't he say earlier that this was the first episode of *Senior Moments* he'd ever worked on?

Earl cleared his throat. "My choice is…bachelorette number two!"

Mrs. Gavelli gave a loud whoop and stood, knocking her table over in the process. She began to jump up and down with excitement as Earl appeared from behind the partition. Their eyes met, and they both froze. The body language said it all.

Mrs. Gavelli pointed a scrawny finger at him. "This guy—*he* most eligible bachelor? Nah. There gotta be some mistake."

Earl's eyes bulged out of his sockets when he saw Mrs. Gavelli. He was about my five-foot-three-inch height, with snow white hair in a comb-over. His sunken face was covered with liver spots that seemed to double in size as he looked her over.

"This is—is—my *date*?" he faltered.

"Yah, that me," Mrs. Gavelli nodded. "Whoo boy, you one lucky son of a gun."

Earl clutched at his chest and slumped to the floor as the closing music of, "Call Me Maybe," filtered through the speakers.

Smiley threw his arms wide open. "See ya' next week folks, on *Senior Moments*!"

CHAPTER FOUR

"Well, at least it wasn't a real heart attack," Josie said. "Earl's granddaughter just put him in her car. The EMTs are gone as well."

"Thank goodness. I'm glad he's all right." I was too exhausted to try and make sense out of all the weirdness from this day. My watch read six fifteen. I had hoped to be home by now. The show business life was not for me.

EMTs had arrived within minutes of Josie calling 9-1-1. Earl had been checked out thoroughly and was declared to be fine. They'd announced that he was suffering from a severe case of indigestion, not a heart attack. Mrs. Gavelli insisted the man was faking, and while Earl lay there, she'd dumped a glass of water over his head to prove her point. She'd almost drowned him in the process.

"At least Nicoletta got what she wanted."

Josie slumped against the table. "Yeah, like always. When Earl said he'd rather die than go to Italy with her, he wasn't kidding. But it's great that he's given up his prize and a sweet deal for Nicoletta. Corey said that she can take whoever she wants. Will your grandmother go?"

"Who else would put up with her?" I scoffed. "I believe they're going to wait until the end of summer to leave. September is a great month to visit Italy. But I don't know how my family will manage without her for ten whole days." Heck, we couldn't get along without Grandma Rosa for even *one* day.

"It will do your parents good," Josie said wisely. "They're too dependent on her. Rosa needs a vacation, although I wouldn't call going anywhere with Nicoletta a vacation."

I took a sponge and wiped down the table. "I wish she hadn't been subjected to all that smut. It was degrading."

"Don't worry," Josie assured me. "They'll cut out all the

bad parts before it airs."

I stared at her in surprise. "But then there wouldn't be any footage left. It was a total disaster."

"Who cares?" Josie laughed. "Your grandmother gets to go back to her beloved birth country, and it will be great exposure for the bakery. Wait and see."

"I hope you're right."

"Rosa's a grown woman, Sal. She knew exactly what she was doing. She cares about Nicoletta and wants to do this for her friend. They'll have a fabulous trip. It's been a long while since they've both been to Italy." Josie picked up her purse and scanned the area one last time. Satisfied that everything was in its proper place, she turned to me. "Do you mind if I head out? Rob's going into work a little earlier tonight, so I need to get home. I didn't think I'd be here this late."

"No, go ahead. I'll wait until everyone's gone." I glanced at my watch again. Cookie would be going to bed soon. Oh well. As the owner, it was only right that I stay behind. Besides, Josie was opening in the morning.

Josie peeked through the doors into the storefront. "Who's left out there?"

"Slim's around somewhere, and I think Smiley's still upstairs in the apartment. He was calling it his dressing room."

"Give me a break." Josie slung her purse over her shoulder. "See you in the morning, girlfriend."

After she'd left, I locked the back door and went into the storefront. With a sigh, I stared across the street at my new house. Mike was probably giving Cookie her bath and then would read her a story. She especially loved the Clifford ones and would shout, "Book!" after her bath. If we were both home, Mike and I would act out the different characters in the story for her, with Mike doing all the male voices, including Clifford. I sighed.

My thoughts were interrupted by a loud, angry voice that I recognized as Smiley's coming from upstairs. I paused to listen.

"I don't understand what you want from me," Smiley said. Silence followed for a few seconds and then, "I told you, I don't have it."

An icy chill wafted down my spine. Before I could react, a door slammed and Slim hurried down the stairs, taking them two at a time. He slowed his pace when he caught sight of me.

"Is everything okay?" I asked.

He gave a curt nod. "Yeah. It's all good. Um, everything's out of here, and I'll be on my way. Smiley should be down any minute. Corey said to tell you that the station will send your money in a couple of weeks."

"Thanks. It was nice meeting you."

Slim avoided my eyes as he slung a backpack over his shoulder. "Thanks for your patience. See ya."

After he'd left, I locked the front door and removed the *Closed for Taping* sign. Back to normal life tomorrow. I went out into the kitchen and searched my purse for my keys. They weren't there. Mystified, I glanced around the kitchen. What the heck? Cookie must have taken them again. Oh well. I could lock the doors but would have to come back later to set the alarm. At least my house was within walking distance.

I decided it was time to hurry Smiley along. What was he still doing up there anyway? I climbed the stairs and was about to knock on the door when it flew open, knocking me to the floor.

Smiley helped me up. "Are you all right, Mrs. Donovan? Gee, I'm sorry. I didn't mean to startle you."

I tried to regain my composure. "I'm fine. Sorry. I—I just came upstairs to see if you—"

He looked embarrassed. "Oh, right. My apologies. You're probably waiting for me to leave so that you can go home."

"Yes, but there's no rush." Shoot. Why did I say that? I didn't want Smiley lingering around the bakery anymore. *Stupid, stupid.* I was flustered and preoccupied with thinking about the earlier conversation I'd overheard. Had he been talking to Slim or someone on the phone?

It seemed odd that a big star like Smiley would be the last one to leave after the taping. He must have better things to do. I couldn't help but notice that his face was as white as a ghost, and there were dark circles of weariness underneath his eyes. The stage makeup had done a fine job of hiding them earlier. He flashed me his trademark grin, but it no longer lit up the room. His right hand, which clasped a manila envelope, started to shake uncontrollably.

"Are you okay?" I asked.

Smiley ignored my question. "Let me get my stuff, and I'll leave." He picked up his phone, and shoved it into a small suitcase, then turned out the light and closed the door behind him. Smiley led the way down the stairs, with me on his heels. When we reached the bottom step, he moved the envelope to his left hand and held the right one out to me. His grin seemed forced.

"You don't look well," I said honestly.

Smiley tried to grin but failed miserably. "Gee, thanks."

"Sorry, that came out wrong. I only meant that you look tired. Maybe you're working too hard?" I suggested.

He shook his head. "No, everything's fine. I just need to figure out how to deal with something. A personal issue."

Now my curiosity had really piqued. "Is there anything I can do to help?"

"No, but thanks."

"Would you like a cup of coffee and a cookie before you leave?" Me and my big mouth. Why, oh why, did I say that?

Smiley looked surprised but grateful. "Thanks, that would be great. I could use one. But I'll take it to go so I don't hold you up any longer, Mrs. Donovan."

"Please call me Sally." I went behind the front counter and opened the drawer underneath the Keurig. "Would you like regular or decaf?"

"Regular would be great. I take it black, please." Smiley seemed more at ease than before. "These days, I need all the caffeine I can get."

"Yeah, I can relate."

Smiley stared with interest at the cookies in the display case. He pointed at the tray of fortune cookies. "Well, since I like anything that has to do with gambling and fate, I'll take one of those."

"Sure thing." I placed a cover on the to-go cup and handed it to him, along with a fortune cookie that had been dipped in chocolate and sprinkles. Smiley placed the envelope and coffee cup on the table where Mrs. Gavelli had been sitting earlier. He snapped open the fortune cookie and his smile faded..

My heart sank. *Oh, no. Please, not another lousy fortune.* "What does it say?"

He held up the two broken pieces. "Nothing. There's no message inside."

"Oh, dear. I'm terribly sorry about that. I must have left it out by mistake." It had to be me. Josie would never have been that careless. Her baking skills were always perfect.

Smiley waved a hand dismissively. "No problem." He popped a piece of cookie into his mouth and tucked the other one into the pocket of his blazer. With a grin, he reached into his pants pocket and drew out a deck of cards. "When I said I was a gambling man, I meant it. Do you play?"

"Not professionally," I teased, but Smiley didn't seem to get the joke. "Actually, I learned to play poker when I was a kid. My parents used to have weekly games at their house." Mom, Dad, and Grandma Rosa had played, sometimes Mrs. Gavelli, and another family from our neighborhood. Sometimes the games would last until three o'clock in the morning. Nowadays my parents were too busy for such extracurricular activities.

Smiley held up a seven of diamonds. "Did you know that each card has a different meaning?"

Again, I glanced at my watch. Cookie might already be asleep. "No, I didn't. Are you talking about Tarot cards?"

"No, regular playing cards." Smiley held up a three of diamonds. "For example, this card means trouble. When you think about it, these cards are sort of like your fortune cookies. They each tell a different story. And they always come true."

A chill wafted down my spine. No, this was silly. Playing cards and fortune cookies could not predict the future. I tried to change the subject. "It must be exciting to be a TV star."

Smiley placed the deck back in his pocket and picked up the coffee cup. "Honestly? At first, yes. But the magic is gone now."

I didn't know what to say to that.

Smiley took a sip of coffee. "This is perfect, thanks. Hot and bitter, just like me."

"Excuse me?" I asked.

His grin disappeared. "Sorry, that was meant to be a joke. But you don't know me, so there's no way you'd understand the pun." Smiley heaved a long sigh. "It's these long hours, you understand. Sometimes they mess with your health and personal life."

"It must be tough on your family as well," I added.

A shadow passed over Smiley's face. "I don't have any kids. It's only my wife and me." Now it was his turn to try and change the subject. "Did you know that I grew up in the Buffalo area?"

"Yes, I heard you say so during the taping."

Smiley produced a pen from his blazer pocket. "That's why I kept asking for a show to be done in this area. When the network received Mrs. Gavelli's letter, it was a no brainer. I told the executives we were doing it, no matter what. Hey, give me your address, and I'll send you an autographed photo."

I recited it for him, even though I wasn't interested in his photo. Maybe Josie would like it. "What a small world."

He grinned. "Isn't it? I own a house in Rochester but still like coming here. It brings back a lot of good memories."

"Rochester's a nice city," I commented. "Is your wife with you on this trip?"

Smiley picked up the envelope from the table, averting his eyes. "Um, actually, no. We're separated. It's a long tedious story that I won't attempt to bore you with."

Well, this was awkward. "I'm very sorry."

He gulped down the rest of his coffee. "It's fine, really. Angela filed for divorce months ago, but it's not official yet. I've learned that life goes on, no matter what. Anyway, I'm sorry for keeping you. Do you live far from here?"

"No." I pointed at the window. "Right across the street."

Smiley followed my gaze. "Wow, very nice. That must make it convenient to come to work.

"Very," I laughed.

Smiley tossed the coffee cup in the trash and extended his other hand for me to shake. When I touched his fingers, I recoiled. They were as cold as icicles. He opened his mouth as if to say something then shut it quickly.

"Are you sure that you're feeling okay?" It was obvious there was something wrong with the man.

He hesitated but shook his head. "It's all good. You've been very kind. I'd better get back to the hotel. We have another show to tape tomorrow. This one is over the Canadian border. After that, I get a few days off."

"Are you sure?"

Smiley's trademark grin appeared from out of nowhere, even though his eyes seemed to be crying out for help. "Nothing a good night's sleep won't cure. Thanks again for your hospitality. Oh, and if you'd be so inclined, please let Rosa, Nicoletta and Dodie know that the show will probably air in a couple of weeks. The station will be in touch to let everyone know the exact date."

"Sounds good."

I waited while he walked outside and climbed into an older SUV parked at the curb. I'd expected to see him driving something flashy, like a BMW or Lamborghini. Smiley started the engine and let the car idle. Every few seconds, he would glance back over to see if I was still watching him. His behavior troubled me, but I wasn't sure why. Smiley seemed hesitant to leave, and I was growing impatient. There were more important things for me to do than wait around until he left. I shut off the lights, locked the front door, and hurried across the street, not even bothering to look back.

With Smiley out of sight and mind, I took a moment to admire the new beige colonial before me. It was more than twice the size of our former home. My husband's talent never ceased to amaze me. The colonial was set far back from the road, on approximately half an acre. We needed to plant grass seed around the house and do some landscaping, but I could already picture how lovely it would look next summer.

Our old house wasn't empty yet, and we needed to work on putting it up for sale. The money would desperately help with our new mortgage. Mike didn't seem to be in a hurry, and I suspected he felt guilty about selling the place. Although his memories of growing up in the house had been painful, it was still the last link he had with his mother. She'd died before I returned to Colwestern.

For me, the best part about our new home was the backyard. Our former lawn had been about the size of a handkerchief, but this time around, there was room for everything I'd wanted. Land was not an easy commodity to come by in Colwestern. Mike had installed a four-foot-tall classic white picket fence around the entire house. We didn't want to take any chances that Cookie might wander out the front door and into the road.

Out back was a sandbox I'd already bought for Cookie, plus a little wading pool. My new patio furniture was scheduled to arrive later next week, and I'd ordered a gas grill as a Father's Day present for Mike. We were looking forward to barbecuing all summer long.

When I walked through the entranceway, the pitter patter of little feet could unmistakably be heard.

"Mama!" Cookie ran toward me from the kitchen, her arms open wide. "Kiss, kiss!"

My heart melted at the sight of her. Cookie was all ready for bed, dressed in her pink cotton pajamas. Her curly black hair was still damp from her bath. I picked her up in my arms and hugged her against me. She smelled wonderful, of baby lotion and shampoo. "Here's my precious girl. What have you been doing?"

"Pike," she sputtered and pointed at the black and white Shih Tzu, who trotted in from the kitchen. She wriggled out of my arms and toddled over to pat him on the back, but it was more like a slap. "Doggie. Mine."

Spike was nearly sixteen but still active for his age. Mike had adopted him from a shelter when he was a puppy. He was fiercely protective of us and considered Cookie his special playmate. He didn't even flinch when she tugged on his fur.

"No, no. Don't hurt Spike. Nice and gentle." I took her hand and guided it down Spike's back. "That's a good girl."

Mike appeared in the hallway, a can of soda in his hand. He put an arm around my shoulders and kissed me. "I fed Cookie but figured I'd wait until you got home so we could eat together."

"That sounds great. I'm starved." We went into the kitchen, our arms around each other, with Cookie and Spike trailing after us.

"Nom nom," Cookie announced, and tried to climb into her highchair.

Mike laughed and lifted the tray then placed her in the seat. "You can't be hungry again, silly. You just ate before your bath."

Cookie grunted in response. As I helped myself to fried rice and an egg roll, she watched with large, round blue eyes and banged her little fist on the highchair tray.

"She's always hungry," I said between bites. "She must be going through another growth spurt." I wished that I could use the same excuse for myself.

"Eat," Cookie said wisely and grabbed a piece of sesame chicken from her tray.

"By the way, young lady." I tried my best to act stern with her. "Where are Mama's keys?"

Cookie accepted a piece of chopped up eggroll from Mike. "No. No key."

Mike dumped a spoonful of fried rice into Cookie's Peter Rabbit bowl. "Did she take them again?"

"Yep. I had to walk home from the bakery. I need to go back over and set the alarm."

"I thought you could just punch the code in," Mike said.

"Not with the new system. This was Josie's idea, remember? She said we'd save money in the long run." I turned my attention back to my daughter. "Tell Mommy what you did with the keys, baby."

Cookie pressed her lips together in a stubborn manner and shook her head. "No. Key."

Mike heaped sweet and sour pork onto his plate. "Don't keep me in suspense, Sal. You said in your text that Earl had a heart attack when he saw Mrs. Gavelli. Is he okay?"

I swallowed a bite of my sesame chicken before answering. "He's fine. It was indigestion, not a heart attack. Then Mrs. Gavelli dumped a glass of water over his head to prove he was all right. Earl got up, announced that she could have both tickets to Italy, and got out of the bakery as fast as he could."

Mike chuckled as he munched on an egg roll. "Can you imagine sitting next to that woman on an airplane for eight hours?"

"More, Dada. More!" Cookie shouted.

I laughed at her enthusiasm, but decided that she should have something healthier. I went to the fridge and grabbed an apple, then sliced it up into small pieces. "She's getting more like my father every day."

"Papa." Cookie stared around the room hopefully and giggled. Papa was the name that she called my father. In Cookie's book, he and my mother always delivered a fun time.

"Papa will be home soon," I said.

Mike placed an apple piece on Cookie's highchair tray. "So, what's Nicoletta going to do for a traveling companion?"

"She's taking my grandmother with her." I leaned back in the chair and put my feet up on the empty one next to it. The day had turned out to be much longer than I'd anticipated. I told Mike about everything that had gone wrong, how Corey shouted himself hoarse, and how Dodie said she wouldn't be in to work tomorrow. She needed a day to recuperate.

He laughed out loud. "There's only one thing that would have made the day worse."

"That's impossible. It couldn't have been any worse."

"You're forgetting about your parents," Mike pointed out. "If they had been at the bakery, you'd still be there, trying to finish up. By the way, when are they coming home?"

"Their flight gets in tomorrow at noon," I said. "Cookie will see Papa and Grammy tomorrow."

Cookie's face lit up. "Papa!" she giggled. "Fun."

"Yep, that's one way to look at it," Mike agreed.

"I felt so sorry for my grandmother. She didn't want to be on the show. I keep hoping that something will happen so it never gets televised."

"Your grandmother is as tough as they come," Mike said. "She always knows exactly what she's doing. Rosa only wants to make everyone happy. If not with food, then something else. Nicoletta may be a pest, but your grandmother loves her anyway."

"Someone has to." I leaned over to give him a kiss. "I love you and our baby girl."

"More!" Cookie banged her spoon on the tray.

"Here, baby." I gave her the rest of the apple pieces and watched as Cookie quickly scarfed them up. "Jeez. Did Johnny even feed her today?"

Mike nodded. "He said that she ate Cheerios, applesauce, chicken nuggets, and a banana. By the way, Johnny said that Cookie hid his keys from him. Sounds like she might have a problem."

My little angel was turning into a kleptomaniac. "All right, young lady." Once again, I tried to act serious, but it was difficult when she had rice all over her chin. I laughed out loud and wiped the mess off her with a clean washcloth. "Tell Mama what you did with her keys."

Again, she shook her head. "No. Keys."

I got up from the table and went into the living room. Mike had left the diaper bag on the couch, and I rapidly sorted through the contents. There were unused diapers, baby powder, an empty sippy cup, change of clothes, and Cookie's plush Clifford toy. No keys anywhere. I checked under the cushions of the couch, which were another favorite hiding place of hers. Nothing.

"Honey, check Spike's bed, will you?" I called out to Mike. The doggie bed was located on the floor of the laundry room, which adjoined the kitchen. It was convenient for Cookie since she was only a couple of feet tall.

After checking the couch, I ran upstairs and looked in Cookie's bedroom. Her crib and dresser were the only furniture in here so far. We hadn't moved the rocking chair and most of her toys over from the old house yet. The room was spacious, with thick shag beige carpeting. Mike had painted it pink, with white clouds on the ceiling. There was still more I wanted to do, but it was a great start.

There were no keys in the bottom drawer of the dresser, but I did find a lipstick that belonged to my mother, one of my father's bookmarks, and my oven timer. Good grief. This kid was slicker than our driveway during a winter ice storm.

I hurried back down the stairs. Cookie was out of her highchair and chasing Spike around the living room. I tried to lift her into my arms. "You have to tell Mama where you put the keys, baby."

"No!" she shouted and wriggled out of my grasp. "No, no. Keys!"

With a sigh, I glanced around the room. There were still several storage boxes stacked against the wall, but they were all taped up. Even with Cookie's special talent, there was no way that she could get inside. The only other furniture in the high beamed ceiling room was a flatscreen TV, recliner, and desk. We had a sectional on order that was coming next week.

Mike was still in the kitchen, cleaning up the floor where Cookie had thrown the last of her fried rice. "No luck," I said. "You still have the spare key with the alarm fob, right?"

Mike reached into the kitchen drawer and produced an impressive ring of keys from it. He removed the fob and key and placed them in my hand. "You'd better not wait," he advised. "With your luck, someone will try to break in tonight."

Perhaps I should have been insulted, but Mike spoke the truth. Sally's Samples had been vandalized before, and I wasn't about to take any more chances. "I'll run across the street, set the alarm, and come right back. Wait for me so that we can read to Cookie together, okay?" It was my favorite time of the day—being with the ones that I loved most in this world.

"Of course." He nuzzled his lips against mine. "And after she's asleep, we'll have some quiet Mommy and Daddy time."

"Can't wait." I kissed him and hurried out the front door.

Even though the bakery was only across the street, it was situated in a commercial zone while our house was in a residential one. The colonial was set far enough back from the road so that we were not concerned about traffic noise from the two-lane road. I turned and glanced back at the house with pride. The only thing left was to fill the empty bedrooms with more children, which we both desperately wanted.

I jogged down to the road, looked both ways, and sprinted across. When I went to insert my key into the hole, the door edged forward. Holy cow. What was going on? I was positive I'd locked it. Then again, I was awfully forgetful these days. Proceeding with caution, I pushed it open farther and clicked on the light.

"Hello?" My voice echoed through the empty room.

There was no sign of anything being disturbed. The bakery looked exactly the same as when I'd left it earlier. No signs from the earlier filming remained, and the tables had all been returned to their normal positions. My gleaming display case, which was polished daily, held a few cookies that Josie had baked early this morning, before the taping. The cherry almond ones were a new addition, and the recipe created by yours truly. It was the first recipe I'd ever created all by myself. I would never get close to Josie's level of culinary skills, but I'd still come a long way, baby.

My eyes flickered down to the floor. There was an object lying near the case, in front of the door that led to the kitchen. With trepidation, I approached it and stared down. A broken piece of fortune cookie lay there. My heart skittered inside my chest. The cookie hadn't been there when I'd left. Was this the piece Smiley had put in his pocket earlier? He'd eaten the other half in front of me.

No. Of course it wasn't the same cookie.

A chill washed over me. Where had the cookie come from? *No, no. Stop it, Sal.* I was letting my imagination run away with me, but a little voice from within screamed that something was desperately wrong with this scenario. I pulled my phone out and dialed 9-1-1, my finger hovering over the Send button, just in case. With a deep breath, I pushed open the kitchen door and looked inside.

The room was covered with a coating of flour. It looked as if Betty Crocker and Julia Child had been involved in some kind of wrestling match. The cookie rack lay on its side, the empty trays spilled out all over the floor. Footprints dotted the flour tracks on the tile floor, and I spotted a handprint on the wooden block table. My rolling pin was next to the print, covered in what looked like blood.

Dizziness swept over me, and I dropped the phone, vaguely aware of the cracking sound it made against the floor tiles.

On the other side of the tipped over rack lay a man's body. He was positioned on his back, and vacant brown eyes were open and staring unseeing into space.

The trademark grin was gone, but there was no doubt about it. Smiley Jones had returned to my bakery, and someone had made sure that he would never leave again.

Spots danced before my eyes as I opened my mouth and let out a loud, terrified scream.

CHAPTER FIVE

My hands shook as I tried to balance a cup of water between them. I wanted to tell myself that Smiley's murder had been a figment of my imagination, or that I was simply so exhausted I'd dreamed the entire thing. No matter how often I found a dead body, I would never get used to it.

I couldn't believe this was happening again and in, of all places, my bakery. This was my happy place, my comfort zone. Josie and I spent several hours a day here creating delectable treats for customers. How could I go about business as usual without seeing visions of Smiley's lifeless body everywhere?

One thing was for certain. I would never look at a rolling pin in the same manner again.

Officer Fred Walden was in his early twenties, with a baby smooth face that made me wonder if he'd even started shaving yet. He smiled reassuringly at me from across the table. "Can you go on, Mrs. Donovan, or do you need another moment?"

"I'm okay." It would be better to get this over with as soon as possible.

He checked the notes on his pad. "What time did you say you arrived at the bakery?"

"Um, I left my house at about seven thirty." I took a sip of water and exhaled sharply. "I live across the street, so it only took me a couple of minutes to get here and…find him."

Although I knew most of the Colwestern Police Department, I'd never met Officer Walden before. He must be new to the force. I tried to concentrate on what he'd said, but it was difficult. My mind was too preoccupied with memories of Smiley's bloodied face. It would haunt me for many nights to come.

Officer Walden tapped his pen against his teeth and

stared over my shoulder at a couple of uniformed policemen and a man from forensics. The medical examiner had removed Smiley's lifeless body and taken it away in his van. A few nosy spectators remained outside. As usual, my bakery was a source of talk and amusement in the town. Even though I couldn't hear what they were saying, I *knew* what was being said. *Oh, yes. You heard right, Matilda. Sally Donovan found another dead body. How many does that make now?*

The man from forensics had finished taking photos of the kitchen with his camera and I could hear him speaking in a low tone to one of the other officers. The process was all too familiar to me but one thing, or rather, one person was missing.

A deep male voice spoke from behind me. "Well, Sally. We meet again. I kind of thought we might be done with all of this. Or at least I'd hoped so."

I winced, recognizing the voice immediately. Brian Jenkins stood there, hands on hips, shaking his head at me. Instead of his usual police uniform, Brian was dressed in a striped navy and white dress shirt with navy slacks. His dirty-blonde hair was damp, as if he'd recently gotten out of the shower.

"Hi, Brian." Officer Walden greeted him. "I thought you were off tonight."

"Do any of us ever really get a night off, Fred?" Brian smiled, but the grin faded when our eyes met. "Sally's an old friend, so I can take over."

Officer Walden's chair scraped against the floor as he pushed it back. "Sure thing. I'll see if there's something else that I can help with around here." He politely tipped his hat at me and went into the kitchen.

Brian turned the vacant chair around and sat down, his hands resting on its back. "Fred's only been with the force for a few weeks. We need to break him in gradually. He's not ready for you yet, Sally."

"Gee, nice to see you too."

Brian's green eyes, flecked with gold, appraised me in silence for a few seconds. "You look tired."

"So do you."

He smiled. "My son was up all night with an earache, and I've got more than a few crimes to solve in this town. Oh, wait, let's add a murder to the list. Your timing is lousy, you know."

Good grief. "Jeez, Brian, it's not like I'm the one who

killed him. And for the record, I'm not too happy about it either. The man died in *my bakery*. What's this going to do to my business? And why are you tackling all these cases anyway? Doesn't the police force have detectives to handle that?"

Brian held up a lone finger. "Yes, they do—a total of one now. This is my second week in the job."

"Wow, I hadn't heard that." Brian mentioned last year that he had taken the detective's exam, but until now I'd forgotten all about it. "Congratulations."

"Thanks, I think." He picked up Officer Walden's pen. "Okay, talk to me. Why was Smiley Jones in your bakery—all alone? Did you let him in and then leave?"

I rolled my eyes at him. "Of course not. He left before I locked the door. I saw him get into his vehicle."

Brian's eyes clouded with suspicion. A handsome man with a Greek god–like profile, he'd been interested in me romantically when we first met five years ago, shortly after the bakery opened. Brian had been the first policeman to arrive on the scene when my high school nemesis had dropped dead at my former bakery's location. While I'd liked him immediately, my heart had always belonged to Mike.

When I met Brian, ten years had passed since my breakup with Mike at our senior prom. Time didn't matter, though. I had never stopped loving him, and he felt the same about me. We reunited shortly after my return to Colwestern. As Grandma Rosa often said, "Some things are just meant to be, *cara mia*."

"But I don't understand," Brian said. "How could Smiley be in your bakery if you left before him? You locked the door, right?"

I was starting to lose patience. "Jeez, Brian. If I didn't know any better, I'd say that you were insulting my intelligence. Of course, the door was locked. I wasn't able to set the alarm because my keys were lost, so I went home and came back with an extra fob. That's when I found Smiley."

"How long were you gone?" Brian wanted to know.

"About an hour—maybe a little less."

Brian made a note on the pad Officer Walden had left behind. "There doesn't appear to be any signs of breaking and entering. How else could he have gotten in?"

"Excuse me, Mrs. Donovan?" Officer Walden walked back over to us. In his gloved hand was a ring of keys. "These were found in Mr. Jones's pants pocket. Are they yours?"

Goosebumps dotted my arms as I stared at the keys. There was no doubt about it. A miniature silver frame with a photo of Mike, Cookie, and me dangled from the middle of the ring. Cookie had told the truth after all—she hadn't taken them.

"Um, yes," I sputtered. "But I don't know how he got them."

I reached for the ring, but Brian shook his head. "Sorry, Sally. We need to keep these as evidence for now."

"Oh, sure. Right." I should have remembered.

Brian stared at me thoughtfully, as if trying to figure me out. "Why do these things keep happening to you? No offense, Sally, but you're like some type of murder magnet."

"You're full of compliments tonight. By the way, how are Ally and Ling?" Ling was the baby that Brian and his wife had adopted. He was only a few months younger than Cookie.

Brian shifted in his seat. "Everyone's fine, thanks. Ally said to tell you hello."

Ally Jenkins had been a high school classmate of mine. She worked as a nurse at Colwestern Hospital and had once mistaken me for competition of Brian's affections. Fortunately, that was all in the past now.

"Well, I'm so glad we've had a chance to catch up." The sarcasm was obvious in my tone.

Brian's face flushed. "Look, I'm sorry. It's just kind of creepy how you always manage to be in such close proximity to every murder in our town. What am I missing here? Why was Smiley even in Colwestern?"

"He filmed an episode of *Senior Moments* in my bakery today. My grandmother and Nicoletta were contestants, along with Dodie." I quickly explained to him how it had all happened.

Brian shook his head. "Okay, something's really wrong here. Your grandmother was on a reality dating show? I'm having a little trouble believing that."

"Yeah, you're not the only one. She only did it to appease Mrs. Gavelli. In the end, it all worked out. Both of them are going on a trip to Italy."

Brian stroked his clean-shaven chin. "Good for them. Now, tell me about the eligible bachelor, Earl Jacobsen. Fred's notes said that he almost had a heart attack when he found out Nicoletta was going to Italy with him. I mean, that could give anyone a fit. Could he have blamed Smiley and then come back to harm him?"

"Doubtful. Earl could barely walk when he left here. There's no way he could have returned and attacked Smiley with the rolling pin." My mouth went dry as realization set in. My rolling pin had been responsible for a man's death. A crime of passion with uncontrollable rage. Who could have hated Smiley that much?

Brian watched me with an anxious expression. "Are you sure that you're okay?"

"Not really." I licked my lips. "I realize now that it was a mistake to let them film a show in my bakery. This is the first time a murder has ever happened here." My former location was a different story. A dead body had been found inside after a fire had started, and the building needed to be demolished afterwards. For a long time, I'd had no idea how the deceased man had gotten inside. It was similar to this situation but altogether different.

Smiley had seemed like an affable guy to me. Sure, he'd been a bit edgy and impatient while they were filming, but a day with Mrs. Gavelli could do that to anyone.

Officer Walden opened his gloved hand to reveal a small plastic bag with a deck of cards inside. "This was in Smiley's other pocket."

"Smiley showed me the cards while we were talking," I explained. "He said something about being a gambling man and that the cards all had different meanings."

Brian ran his fingers over the plastic and addressed the officer. "Did you notice anything odd about them?"

Officer Walden nodded. "Kind of. There's a couple of cards missing. One is the ace of spades."

My jaw dropped. "Doesn't that card mean death?"

"How appropriate," Brian murmured.

A noise from the kitchen startled us, and a second later Josie appeared. "Sal!" She flew across the room to our table.

Officer Walden stopped her before she reached me. "I'm sorry, ma'am. This is a crime scene. You'll have to wait outside."

Brian held up a hand. "It's okay, Fred. This is Josie Sullivan. She works here with Sally, and I have questions for her as well."

Officer Walden nodded and left us alone.

Josie pulled up a chair and sat down beside me. "Dylan

had a baseball game, so I didn't see your text until we got home. God, I hate it when they play those games in rural areas. My phone absolutely refuses to work." She glanced around the room. "Where's Mike? I thought he'd be here."

"I told him to stay home with Cookie." It was reassuring to know my husband was only across the street if I needed him, and I didn't want to subject Cookie to a crime scene. Even though she was only eighteen months old, I worried that it could leave some kind of lasting impression upon her.

Josie snorted. "I'll bet he had a few things to say."

"Oh, did he ever." After I'd assured him that I was okay, Mike's reaction had been one of disbelief. He wanted to know why these things kept happening to me, and I couldn't give him a straight answer.

Officer Walden cleared his throat. "Detective, I just received word that the rest of the television crew for *Senior Moments* is on their way to the precinct for questioning. I know it's your day off, but if there's any way you could—"

"Glad to help out," Brian cut in. "I'd already planned on it."

"I don't believe this," Josie murmured. "Who could have wanted to kill him? Smiley seemed like a nice guy. And the public certainly loved him."

Brian leaned back in his seat. "You ladies should know by now that people are not always what they seem."

His words unnerved me. "What exactly are you saying, Brian? What was going on with Smiley?"

"Did he have an alias?" Josie asked. "Was he living a double life?"

Brian tapped his pen against the table. "Not in the way that you think."

"You're confusing me," I said. "Come on, let's have it. What kind of skeletons did Smiley have in his closet?"

Brian narrowed his eyes at us. "He killed someone."

CHAPTER SIX

I crumpled the plastic cup between my hands. The few remaining drops of water inside it shot up and splashed me in the face, but I barely noticed. "This is some kind of a joke, right?"

Josie shook her head. "You've been working too hard, Brian. Smiley was in the public eye all the time. People across the country adored him. There's no way he could be a killer."

Brian's mouth tightened. "Thank you for your faith in me, Josie, but let me assure you, I have my facts straight. Smiley Jones was responsible for the death of another person."

"What happened?" I asked.

"He was leaving a party in Rochester, about three years ago," Brian explained. "Smiley had a little too much cocaine in his system, and there's no way he should have been operating a moving vehicle. He hit a car with two women inside. The driver died instantly, and the other woman was left paralyzed."

"How awful," I muttered. "Did he do any jail time?"

Brian's expression was one of disgust. "None."

"What?" Josie exploded. "How is that even possible?"

"Because he had enough money to buy his way out," Brian said. "It seems he settled out of court with both parties for the civil suit, and there was a plea agreement with the district attorney's office. The deceased victim's husband agreed to accept a lump sum payment from Smiley. Her parents were against it, but the husband still went ahead and took the money, then moved to Canada."

"What about the other victim?" Josie asked. "The woman who was paralyzed?"

Brian ran a hand through his dirty-blond hair. "She received her money and relocated out west with her family. A year after the accident, she died of breast cancer."

"That's awful," I lamented. "Those poor women."

"Your favorite game show host did some community service to show how sorry he was." Brian's tone was bitter. "Everything got swept under the rug, so to speak. Smiley was back to his phony television career within six months."

"Cripes," Josie muttered. "There are some serious problems with our judicial system."

"Also," Brian went on, "his name wasn't Smiley Jones. That's just a name he uses for TV. His real name was Jonas Jones."

Josie tried her best to hold back a snort but failed miserably.

"It's not funny," I said. "The man is dead."

"Seriously?" Josie shook her head. "Wow. That's as bad as having your parents name you Donald when your last name is Duck."

"No, not as bad," Brian said. "But close."

I kept silent. My first husband, Colin Brown, had been a verbally abusive jerk whom I never should have wed. If that wasn't bad enough, I'd taken constant ribbing about my new last name during our entire marriage. The name didn't go very well with Sally, and people always asked how my brother Charlie and his friend Linus were doing. It got old fast.

"Sally, just so you're aware, I will have questions for your grandmother, Nicoletta, and Dodie as well," Brian continued.

"Oh no," Josie groaned. "More Nicoletta? Like a full day of her wasn't enough already?"

Brian almost smiled. "I don't see the harm in waiting until tomorrow to talk to all three of them."

This was a relief. I too had heard and seen enough of Nicoletta for one day and was certain that my grandmother must be exhausted. I rose from the table. "Is there anything else? I'd really like to get home to my family."

"No, you both can leave," Brian said. "But you do realize that you can't open for business tomorrow, right?"

"Please tell me you're joking," I said. "How long do we have to stay closed?"

Brian shrugged. "Hard to say. The investigation has to be completed first. This is a messy crime scene that we have on our hands. We need to see if we can locate any DNA—besides Smiley's, that is. It may take a couple of days."

"But this is our livelihood," I protested. "Fridays and

Saturdays are always our busiest days of the week."

"I understand how you feel, but there's nothing I can do about it." Brian's direct gaze met mine. "Try to stay out of trouble for at least a few days, okay?"

* * *

"Gee, we always miss out on the good stuff," my father complained as he poured maple syrup liberally over his cannoli pancakes. He took a large bite, and a piece of syrup-soaked cake fell onto his white T-shirt. Dad muttered something in Italian under his breath. "Gosh darn-it. I can't believe I did that."

"I can." My sister Gianna sat next to me, working her way through a second cup of black coffee. She shook her head at our father. It wouldn't be mealtime at my parents' house if Dad didn't manage to spill something on his clothes. He thoroughly enjoyed his food and ended up wearing it most of the time.

My mother put down her lipstick and compact and immediately dunked her napkin into a glass of water. She began to apply it to my father's shirt. "We're going to have to soak that, honey, or the stain will never come out." Once Mom had finished, she glanced with satisfaction around the table. "It's so good to be back home with my family. The Bahamas were wonderful, but I missed my grandchildren something terrible."

I was convinced that my parents weren't like anyone else's parents. Grandma Rosa affectionately referred to them as nutsy cookies, another one of her mixed-up sayings. Maria Muccio, my fifty-five-year-old mother, enjoyed dressing in clothes that a teenager might wear. Much to mine and Gianna's chagrin, she still shopped at Forever Twenty-One. Mom looked terrific for her age and was often mistaken for my sister, which was hard to take at times.

Domenic Muccio was thirteen years her senior and the proud proprietor of Muccio Mortuary. Dad had possessed a weird obsession with death for as long as I could remember. He'd even written a novel, *How to Plan and Enjoy Your Funeral*. It wasn't the big success he'd hoped for, but it had gotten him enough attention. Dad also had a blog in which he called himself Father Death. He answered questions about funerals and other cheery subjects. He was the Dear Abby of morbid etiquette.

Since I had the day off, I'd offered to go to the airport

with Cookie to pick up my parents, saving Gianna the trouble. The entire family had gathered for brunch at their house afterwards. Grandma Rosa had been cooking up a storm all morning. In addition to the cannoli pancakes, there were sausages, frittatas, fruit, and a breakfast casserole. She'd even made my favorite, her ricotta cheesecake.

Gianna had taken a long lunch break and was currently holding Alex on her lap with one hand and her coffee with the other. Johnny sat at her left. Gianna had left her job as a public defender last year and accepted an offer from one of Colwestern's most prestigious law firms, with a secret hope to make partner in a few years. She had even less spare time than before, and I worried that she was working too hard. My sister was brilliant and beautiful, and I was proud of how far her career had come. She was building quite a reputation as a criminal defense attorney in our town.

"I remember that incident with Smiley Jones," Gianna mused as Alex jumped off her lap. She helped him into the booster seat next to her. "It just goes to show that if you're a celebrity, you can do almost anything and get away with it. Do the police think that someone associated with the fatal car accident might have killed Smiley?"

"It's possible," I admitted. "But according to Brian, everyone associated with the accident has either died or moved away."

Johnny shot me a teasing grin. "Maybe Brian's worried that you're going to take over the investigation once again."

I reached for the plate of pancakes in an attempt to avoid Mike's eyes. "I don't plan to get involved. Maybe the murder happened in my bakery, but that doesn't mean I'll be looking for a killer. That's the police's job."

"Good," Mike said approvingly. "I don't want you involved. Every time I think we're done with this kind of mess, it sneaks right back up on us. Sal, I'm starting to think that you've got a sign on your back that says, 'Dead bodies, walk this way.'"

"Dada!" Cookie interrupted. "Cake!" She banged her chubby little hands on the highchair tray. I sprang into action, chopping up a cannoli pancake for her. Cookie immediately shoved a piece into her mouth. Her eyes grew as round as dinner plates as she ate, and I had to laugh out loud. She giggled back at me, and a small piece of pancake fell out of her mouth and onto the purple flowered shirt she was wearing.

My father beamed with pride as he watched his granddaughter. "That one—she's just like me. A true Muccio, for sure."

"She does remind me of you, Dom, when she eats," Mike murmured and turned his attention back to me. "Something tells me that you're going to end up involved with Smiley Jones's murder."

"Oh. My. God." Gianna was reading something on her phone as my father coughed loudly. She glanced over at him. "Sorry, Dad, but this is important." Our father didn't approve of cell phones at the table.

"What's wrong?" Johnny asked.

Gianna stared at me with pity in her eyes. "I don't believe the audacity of that man."

"Who?" I asked in bewilderment.

She sighed and passed her phone to me. "Guess who mentioned you in his morning newspaper column."

"No way." I gazed at the screen and muttered a curse word in my head. "This can't be happening."

"Let me guess," Mike said. "Our buddy Jerry Maroon is back at it again."

"'Yes, readers, I've got the latest tidbit for you right here. Sally Donovan, Colwestern's very own death magnet, has done it again,'" I read aloud. "'The ever-popular game show host, Smiley Jones, was at Sally's Shambles yesterday to tape an episode of *Senior Moments*. The fortune cookies were so good that Smiley didn't want to leave. And…it turns out that he didn't. Mrs. Donovan found Smiley's lifeless body in her work area last night. Big surprise there!'"

Anger rolled in the bottom of my stomach, but I managed to read on. "'Rumor has it that Smiley was beaten to death with Mrs. Donovan's rolling pin. The woman is baking up another winner as usual! Take my advice, folks. Try another bakery. Stay away. Trust me, Mrs. Donovan is already making a killing without you giving her any more business.'"

Gianna's face became suffused with anger as she took her phone back. "We're going to sue that guy for slander. He can't keep getting away with this crap."

"What about freedom of the press?" Johnny asked.

My father reached for a plate of blueberry muffins that

Grandma Rosa had just set on the table. "That guy abuses his freedom," he muttered. "You'd think he would have learned his lesson after almost getting beaten to death."

Grandma Rosa sat down in an empty chair across from me and shook out her linen napkin. "I would like to think that no one will believe anything that man says. Sally's baked goods speak for themselves."

"Thanks, Grandma. But remember, this is Colwestern. People believe anything that they see in print." I reached for a muffin. They were still warm from the oven, and I was in desperate need of comfort food. "This is going to hurt my business."

My mother trotted around the table on her tiny red stilettos and lifted Cookie out of the highchair. She went back to her seat and perched my daughter on her lap, feeding her a piece of blueberry muffin. "Maybe by the time the bakery reopens, everyone will have forgotten all about it."

"Doubtful." Mike frowned. "That guy will do anything to make the front page. I just wish I knew how he always gets the scoop before anyone else."

Gianna reached for a frittata. "He constantly hangs around the police station. For all we know, he's planted a listening device there."

Grandma Rosa took a muffin and poured herself a cup of coffee from the decanter. "It is such a tragedy. I cannot believe that Mr. Jones is dead. He seemed very nice."

"You make a lot of enemies in that business," my father noted. A sudden gleam came into his eyes. "Hey, Smiley's local, right? Is he going to be buried around here?"

"Really, Dad," Gianna said in disgust.

My father spread his arms out wide. "Hey, you can't blame a guy for trying. I need to make a living too. Having Smiley laid out in Muccio Mortuary would be sure to draw a crowd and maybe some potential customers. Business has been a little slow lately."

"Domenic," my mother warned. "It does seem a little tacky to talk about such things." She swiveled her head in my direction. "Sal, what do you know about Smiley's private life?"

"Nothing besides the car accident," I confessed.

Gianna pushed back her chair. "From what I've read, Smiley Jones had more than a few enemies. After the car accident, people surrounded his house and yelled threats at him. It got so bad that he finally had to move."

"I read that he and his wife had separated." Mom sipped her coffee. "I saw it on Facebook, so you know it must be true."

"Oh right. Smiley did mention that he and his wife were getting divorced and that they had no kids," I said. "He went to school around here, but lives in Rochester…or he did, before they separated."

"Maybe she killed him," my father remarked. "It's always the wife or the butler."

My mother shuddered. "This is getting too depressing. Let's talk about something more cheerful."

"Okay," my father agreed. "I just bought the granddaddy of all coffins. A gold-plated one! Who wouldn't like to be buried in that baby for eternity?"

At that moment, the kitchen door slammed and a voice called out, "Where my baby?"

My father groaned while Gianna's first instinct was to snatch Alex up in her arms. A second later, Mrs. Gavelli appeared in the doorway, holding an envelope in one hand.

Alex's face immediately brightened when he saw her. He got off of Gianna's lap and ran toward her. "Nona!"

Johnny rose from his seat and lifted Alex up so that Mrs. Gavelli could give him a kiss. She patted his dark-brown hair. "Such a good boy. He almost make me feel better about tragedy."

A lone tear trickled down her shriveled cheek. We all stared at her in shock. Mrs. Gavelli did not cry. She had once told my grandmother that it was a sign of weakness. Mesmerized by the sight, I couldn't bring myself to look away.

"Don't worry, Gram," Johnny said. "I'm sure that the police will find Smiley's killer."

Mrs. Gavelli stared at him as if he had corn growing out of his ears. "That not my problem. It not why I upset. People die every day. Hey, it part of life."

"Jeez, woman, the man was murdered," my father said. "It's not like he planned on getting his skull bashed in."

My mother placed her hands over Cookie's ears. "Domenic, that's a terrible thing to say, especially in front of the children."

"Bold," Cookie sang. "Papa. Bold."

"Well, something's obviously happened. Why are you so

upset?" Gianna wanted to know.

Mrs. Gavelli let out a long, piteous sigh. "The TV people call. The trip—she is off. I no get to go to Italy after all."

CHAPTER SEVEN

"You are not making any sense, Nicoletta," Grandma Rosa said quietly. "What do you mean, you cannot go to Italy?"

Mrs. Gavelli sat down heavily in a chair. "The TV station, she just call me. They not gonna air my show till Smiley's killer found. No show, no prize. Why everyone want to take advantage of nice old lady like me?"

My father snorted into his coffee. "Nice? Oh, please. Next to you, Satan is a prince."

"This the contract they make me sign." Mrs. Gavelli waved the envelope under Gianna's nose. Tell me that it all garbage. Then I sue them."

Gianna opened the envelope and began to read the contract to herself. After a minute, she stared up at Mrs. Gavelli and soberly shook her head. "I'm afraid you can't sue them, Nicoletta. They haven't done anything wrong. It's stated right here in paragraph six that they do not have to release the prizes until the episode airs."

"It's the same thing on *Jeopardy*, right?" my father asked. He drummed his fingers on the table, deep in thought. "Oh, wait, maybe not. I think they get to keep the money if you break down and blab to everyone that you won before the episode airs. Yeah, that must be it. You know, I'd have a tough time if I was on that show. Heck, I'd be blabbing it to people all over the place. Can you imagine the booming business Muccio's Mortuary would do after it got out that I had been on *Jeopardy*?"

"Cripes, I don't believe this," Mike murmured.

"Dad," Gianna said sharply. "This isn't the time or place for that." She put the contract back in the envelope and handed it to Mrs. Gavelli. "I'm sorry. I know how much you and Grandma were looking forward to the trip this summer."

Grandma Rosa shrugged. "That is the way the cookie

fumbles."

"Crumbles, Grandma." I couldn't resist putting in my two cents and then immediately clapped a hand over my mouth. "Whoops. I'm sorry. I promised not to correct you anymore."

She patted me on the arm. "It is all right, *cara mia.* You cannot help yourself."

Mrs. Gavelli mumbled under her breath as she poured a cup of coffee from the carafe. "They shameless, that what they are. Who want to keep a sick and feeble woman from going back to country she born in?"

Feeble and sick weren't words that I would use to describe Mrs. Gavelli. We'd all gone on a cruise to the Bahamas last January, and I'd seen firsthand what the woman was capable of. She could easily outrun me and had a mean left hook. In all fairness to her, though, she had been very ill with bone cancer at one time. She'd been in remission for almost four years.

"This may be my last chance to ever go." Mrs. Gavelli clasped her hands together as if in prayer. "I old. I might die soon."

"Yeah, right," my father snickered. "You're too mean to die. You'll be around for at least another fifty years."

Johnny, who had been silent up to now, shot a murderous glance in my father's direction. As usual, it was lost on him. Dad turned his attention back to the food and helped himself to another frittata.

"Gram, there must be something we can do to get you and Rosa to Italy," Johnny said. "I'm sure she wants to go as badly as you do."

"No one want to go as badly as me," Mrs. Gavelli declared.

"How long has it been since you were there last, Grandma?" Gianna asked.

A dreamy look came over Grandma Rosa's face as she stared out the nearby dining room window. "It has been a very long time. I left there with your grandfather when I was only twenty-two. I have always wanted to go back—" She broke off. "But some things are not meant to be."

This was the first time I had ever seen my grandmother so pensive about her own life. She thought daydreaming was a waste of time and didn't believe in being idle. As I watched her, I sensed that she was thinking about something besides Italy.

Perhaps her long-lost love?

Mrs. Gavelli pointed a finger at me. "You gotta find the killer, missy. For me and your grandmama."

"Oh no. Not again," Mike groaned.

"Jerry Maroon—I see him on news this morning." Mrs. Gavelli's eyes gleamed like a cats. "He tell everyone stay away from your bakery. He say it cursed, like you some kind of witch."

"For crying out loud." Dad threw up his hands in disgust.

Mrs. Gavelli examined my face. "You a good girl—for most part. And you find lots of killers. So, you will find this one. There. It all settled."

I loved how she had everything planned out for me. Now what was I supposed to do? Thanks to Jerry and his big mouth, Sally's Samples had received a great deal of negative attention and business might start to decline. Plus, Grandma Rosa and Mrs. Gavelli would lose their trip to Italy if the killer wasn't found soon.

The situation made me feel trapped, like a mouse in a maze. I didn't want to get involved in Smiley's murder, but it was a little too late for that. Brian would be peeved if I meddled in a police investigation. In addition, I had my family to think of, especially my daughter. What would happen when Cookie went to school? Would the kids tease her and say her mother was a death magnet?

There didn't seem to be a way out of this one. I chose my words carefully, praying that Mike wouldn't get upset. "I'll do what I can but can't make any promises."

"Humph," Mrs. Gavelli snorted. "No one go your bakery cause that Jerry say rotten things about you. And I gotta go to Italy. You got no choice."

"Maybe the police have already found Smiley's killer," my mother said hopefully.

Gianna frowned. "It's doubtful. They're overloaded and understaffed these days."

A muscle ticked in Mike's jaw. He started to open his mouth, then thought better of it. But I knew he would have plenty to say when we got home. He finished his breakfast in silence, as an air of gloom settled around us. No matter what I did, someone was going to be upset with me.

Gianna shrugged into her blazer and kissed Alex and Johnny goodbye. "I've got to get back to the office. Sal, I'll run a search on Smiley and let you know what comes up."

"I am not getting involved," I protested.

"Yeah, sure." She leaned over to give me a hug. "No offense, but where have I heard that before?"

* * *

The rest of the day passed uneventfully. Although I was upset about the bakery being closed, we decided to make the most of it and work on the house. Mike finished up some woodworking in the dining room while I busied myself unpacking boxes in the kitchen. Cookie decided that she was going to help and spent most of the afternoon banging pots together on the floor. Poor Spike ran for cover from the noise.

At three o'clock, my phone buzzed. Josie's name appeared on the screen. "Hey."

"Hey yourself." Her voice sounded strained.

"Is everything okay?"

Josie blew out a breath. "Not really. Did you see the article that Jerry the slimeball wrote about the bakery?"

"Yeah, I saw it. Don't worry, Jos. The bakery has made quite a name for itself. No one's going to believe that garbage." It was a good thing that she couldn't see my face.

"Sal, you know better than that," Josie scoffed. "People in this town have nothing else to do than gossip. They believe everything they read in that poor excuse of a newspaper. And that anything Jerry writes is the gospel. There must be something in Colwestern's water."

"Oh, come on. People can't possibly think that the bakery is cursed."

"Three customers have already messaged our Facebook page in the last hour to cancel their orders. Two were for cookies platters, and one was a birthday cake."

Although Sally's Samples was known for its cookies, Josie sometimes made specialty birthday or wedding cakes for customers. She'd attended culinary school after high school and possessed a natural talent for baking and decorating cakes. I was more than happy to give her the opportunity to make some extra money on the side.

Josie's remark made me consider the situation more closely. How could our customers betray us? "Dang. I was hoping we had a few days before we started to see a drop off."

Josie hesitated. "I mean, it wouldn't hurt if we went to talk to Smiley's ex-wife, right? I found her address online."

"You're kidding, right?" I tried to lighten the mood. "Who do you think you are? Me?"

She laughed out loud. "I'm catching on."

"All right." I gave in. "The bakery would probably be closed tomorrow anyway. Maybe Grandma Rosa will watch Cookie for me since Mike has a roofing job."

"We'll only ask her a few questions," Josie said. "Hey, who knows? Maybe we'll even find something out to help the police."

"Yeah, I'm sure Brian will be first in line to thank me," I said sarcastically. "How about we leave at one? I'll drive."

"Works for me," Josie agreed. "If there's time, we can even stop for a late lunch or early dinner. See, this way you can tell Mike we went out to eat and just happened to skip over the rest of the details. Then it wouldn't be a lie."

I couldn't resist a snicker. "Oh, please. He'd see right through it. Mike knows me too well. Besides, I hate lying to him."

"Well, maybe he won't be upset," Josie said thoughtfully. "If we figure out who killed Smiley, maybe Mrs. Gavelli will go to Italy and decide to stay there."

"We couldn't be that lucky. All right, I'll see what I can do. Talk to you later." I clicked off and turned to see Mike standing there, his face etched in suspicion. How long he'd been listening, I wasn't sure, but one thing was for certain. He didn't look happy.

"Ma!" Cookie held out a saucepan. "Cookie. Help."

I reached down and took the pan from her hands. "Thank you, baby."

Mike's eyes searched mine. "Okay, do I even have to ask?"

Cookie held out her arms to me, and I lifted her up. "Josie and I are going to lunch tomorrow."

"And?" he prompted.

Cookie made a grunting sound and pointed at a plate of cookies I'd brought home from the bakery the day before. I reached down to the table and handed her one. "And…we're going to see if we can talk to Smiley's wife."

"Are you kidding?" Mike's jaw dropped. "Sal, I thought you were going to stay out of this mess."

"What can I do?" I asked. "I've got Mrs. Gavelli breathing down my neck, and Jerry's article might ruin my business."

He threw up his hands in disgust. "I don't know, Sal. Some days I just wish that I had a normal life."

"And what exactly does that mean?" I shot back.

Mike's face turned crimson. "Nothing. Forget I said anything."

He couldn't fool me. I knew exactly what he'd been thinking. His life and *wife* were anything but normal.

Mike knew me better than anyone else. We'd only been married for four years but had started dating when I was sixteen. In high school, I knew right away that he was the only man for me. At our senior prom, I became convinced that he had cheated on me and never gave him a chance to explain what had transpired. I'd quickly jumped into another relationship and married Colin while still on the rebound. My marriage to Colin ended when I caught him cheating with my high school nemesis. Shortly after our divorce was finalized, Colin had been murdered.

"Sweetheart, I didn't mean it the way it sounded. But there are times that I'd like to come home to my wife and daughter at the end of the day and not have to worry about you getting shot at, locked in a freezer, or blown to bits by a bomb." Mike's tone was exasperated. "I didn't think that was too much to ask for."

This was the closest we'd been to a fight in two years, before Cookie was born. Tears filled my eyes before I could stop them. "I'm sorry. But I can't sit around and do nothing because—" I stopped midsentence as a wave of dizziness passed over me. I quickly put Cookie down and grabbed the counter.

"Sal, what is it? Are you okay?" Mike placed his arms around my shoulders. "Come on, sit down for a minute." He led me over to the table and pulled out a chair.

"I'll be okay." I didn't want to cause my husband any worry but this was the third time this week I'd had a dizzy spell.

Mike filled a glass with water and handed it to me. "Drink some, baby."

"No!" Cookie banged two pots together. "Cookie. Baby."

"Sal, could you be pregnant?" The gleam of hope in Mike's eyes tugged at my heartstrings.

I shook my head. "The test was negative."

His handsome face grew stern. "Then what else could it be?"

There were a few things that came to mind. Hopefully it was nothing serious. "I have an appointment to see the doctor next week."

"Didn't he say that you were anemic last year? Haven't you been taking iron pills?" Mike asked.

"Not for a while," I admitted. "But I'll start again."

"Good." Mike stared at me worriedly. "Maybe that's all it is."

"I'm sure of it." I said, not feeling sure of anything.

He lifted me from the chair and pulled me into a tight hug. "I'm sorry that we argued, Sal."

"Me too. Are you okay with me going to Rochester tomorrow?" I asked.

Mike sighed. "I guess, as long as you're feeling okay. At least you'll have Josie with you. But I hope this will be the end of your involvement in Smiley's murder."

"You worry too much." I pushed the dark curls off his forehead.

He ran a finger down the side of my cheek. "It's my job to worry about you. Now, go upstairs and lie down for a while. I'll make dinner—with Cookie's help."

"Me." Cookie pointed at herself with obvious approval.

I turned my face into his chest and closed my eyes. "Everything will be fine. Trust me."

CHAPTER EIGHT

Traffic was heavy the next day, and it took over an hour and a half for us to reach our destination in Rochester. Angela Jones lived in a pleasant-looking cul-de-sac, with all of the houses almost identical to each other. They were a few years old and all raised-ranch styles, with two-car garages and neatly trimmed square lawns that had perfect landscaping and picket fences.

Although the neighborhood was for the well-to-do, I'd expected something fancier for Smiley's soon-to-be ex—perhaps even a mansion because of his celebrity status. As I rang the doorbell, I wondered how much money she might stand to inherit from his death. Or had he made someone else the beneficiary? That alone was a great motive for his murder.

A dog barked furiously from inside the house. Josie looked at me with a question in her eyes. "Are we going to tell her we're here to offer our sympathy?"

"No. We'll just tell her the truth."

Josie wrinkled her nose. "I don't think we've ever tried that before."

The door opened a crack, and a woman peered out at us. Tall and slender, she was dressed in jeans and a short sleeved pink blouse. She pushed a strand of baby-fine blonde hair away from her eyes and stared from Josie to me. "Yes?"

"Hi, are you Angela Jones?" I asked.

Her amber colored eyes narrowed. "Are you reporters?"

I choked back a laugh. Josie was wearing her pink Bake My Day T-shirt with cutoff jean shorts, while I had on a short-sleeved tunic and black shorts. We didn't exactly look like we were working for CNN. "No," I assured her.

Angela exhaled sharply. "Good, because I've had my fill of those creeps. They've been harassing me all day. One jerk who works for some nobody newspaper in Colwestern even tried to peer through my window. The next one who tries a stunt like that is going to get arrested for trespassing."

It looked as if Jerry Maroon had beaten us to the punch again. I held out my hand. "My name is Sally Donovan. I own Sally's Samples in Colwestern."

"I don't allow soliciting here." Angela started to close the door.

"We're not selling anything." I waved my hands furiously to get her attention. "My bakery—Sally's Samples—is where your husband was…" I couldn't bring myself to say the word.

Recognition dawned on her face. "Oh! You must be the one who found him."

"Yes, that's right." I gestured at Josie. "This is my friend and business partner, Josie Sullivan. We were wondering if we could talk to you for a minute."

"Why?" Angela's fine arched brows drew together in confusion. "I've already spoken to the police. Look, I'm sorry your bakery had to be the place where Jonas died, but it has nothing to do with me. I'm sure the network will pay for any damages you might have incurred. You're getting nothing from me."

Yikes. A little harsh for a so-called grieving widow.

"That's not why we're here," Josie said.

"Please, it will only take a minute," I pleaded. "And it's very important."

Angela's shoulders slumped forward. "Fine. Whatever." She pushed the door aside and grudgingly allowed us to enter. "I have to be at work in an hour, so you need to make it fast."

We followed her down a narrow hallway with hardwood flooring and past a yellow and white kitchen, where a small terrier began to bark at the sight of us. His paws clawed the baby gate as he repeatedly tried to climb it, but with no success.

"Be a good boy, Jake," Angela said sternly. The dog began to whine at the sound of her voice. "Go lie down in your bed."

To my amazement, the dog obediently trotted over to his padded bed on the floor. He turned around three times and then curled himself into a ball.

Josie's mouth opened. "How do you get him to do that? I can't even teach my dog to roll over."

Thanks to her kids' constant pleading, Josie and Rob had finally given in and adopted a puppy for their sons. Elf was a terrier that the kids had named after their favorite Christmas movie. He was almost a year old and clearly had a mind of his own. He did whatever he pleased, which included clawing holes in the couch and tinkling on the floor. Rob had even taken him to obedience school, but he'd promptly flunked out.

Angela led us to a small but neat living room and gestured towards a black leather sectional. She plopped down across from us in a recliner of the same color and reached for a glass filled with a clear liquid that smelled like Scotch. "You have to show them who's boss. Never let them win. Stand your ground, and if they double cross you, show them the door."

Oh boy. I had a feeling that we were no longer talking about dogs.

"We're very sorry for your loss," I put in.

Angela took a long sip of her beverage and closed her eyes, as if savoring it. "Thanks, but that's not necessary. The divorce would have been final any day now. I've been over Jonas for a long time."

There wasn't much we could say to that.

She glared at me suspiciously over the rim of her glass. "Now I have a question for you two."

"Shoot," I said.

"If you're not reporters, why are you so concerned about Jonas's murder?" Angela asked.

I shifted in my seat. "Because it's created some problems for me—specifically, my bakery."

"Are you deaf?" Angela wanted to know. "I just said that I wasn't paying you any money."

"I'm not here about money, at least not from you. Josie and I want to help find Jonas's killer. The local media is having a field day at my expense, and it's starting to hurt my business." I decided not to mention Mrs. Gavelli and her beloved trip to Italy. A vacation seemed inappropriate to bring up at a time like this. Then again, I was certain that Angela didn't care about the status of my business, either.

She studied me thoughtfully for several seconds, as if trying to figure me out. "No offense, but you two don't exactly look like Sherlock Holmes and Watson. I sympathize with you, honey. I owned a little bakery a long time ago. Jonas insisted that

I give it up when we got married. It was the dumbest thing I ever did—besides marrying him, that is."

Jeez, the woman didn't pull any punches.

"You—ah, said that you were getting divorced?" Josie asked.

"Yes, I filed about nine months ago." Angela checked the time on a diamond-encrusted watch. "It's no secret. The media has had a field day at my expense too."

"Sorry to hear that," I said.

"Don't be." Her voice turned low and husky. "I'm better off without him. Jonas never put me first. We were married for five years. The first two were happy, and then it all went downhill. I was never a priority in his life, but that's what happens when you have an addiction."

I knew only too well what she was talking about. Colin had developed a drinking problem during our marriage, which lead to his untimely murder.

"Was he having an affair?" Josie asked.

Angela shook her head. "No, another woman is something that I could have handled. I'd know what to do in that type of situation. Jonas had a gambling problem. It was out of control."

I'd never understood the addiction myself, but Gianna was a long-time lover of slot machines. After Alex was born, it had become easier for her to stay away, since she never had any time for herself. "Did he like to play the horses?"

"No, Jonas's addiction was poker. He lived to play the game. Seriously, the guy was obsessed. I couldn't compete with a full house or a royal flush."

I thought about the deck of cards he'd shown me at the bakery. "Did Jonas know he had a problem? They say that knowing you have one is half of the battle."

To my surprise, Angela laughed out loud. "Oh, please, honey. Spare me the commercial. Jonas went to Gamblers Anonymous nearly a dozen times, and only because I insisted upon it. He kept promising to change and quit cold turkey if I'd give him one more chance. Blah, blah. Finally, I woke up and threw him out of the house. Jonas had no intention of changing for me or anyone else. He was one of the most selfish jerks who ever lived."

Again, I was at a loss for words. Smiley had seemed like

an affable guy to me the other day, but a ten-minute talk wasn't long enough to reveal his true personality.

"Have I shocked you?" Angela wore a smug smile on her face. "I know that most people think he was this great guy who helped everyone find their soulmate. Nope. Jonas was all about himself and how fast he could throw money away."

"Did he think that someone was out to get him?" I remembered how nervous he had seemed at the bakery, especially after his phone call.

She leaned forward in her chair. "Oh please. He received a few nasty fan mail letters the last couple of years and was ready to go off the deep end. It's all part of being in the public eye. The guy didn't have any thick skin on him."

"Do you still have the letters?" I asked eagerly.

Angela shook her head. "The police asked me the same thing, but Smiley threw them away and pretended like it never happened. He was so good at make believe. Maybe that's why he liked playing cards and then boring everyone with the stupid stories about what each card represented. Do you want to know how much he was addicted? When we were first married, we had a gorgeous Victorian mansion in Rochester and a vacation home in Florida. He spent every Saturday night at the local casino. Once in a while, he'd go on weekdays if he was in the area. Smiley thought nothing of dropping twenty grand in one night."

"Holy cow," Josie breathed.

"You see this house?" Angela spread her arms open. She was clearly on a roll now. "Jonas owed so much money to bookies that we were forced to sell our mansion and could barely afford a down payment on this one. One night when he was down about fifty grand, he decided to put up the deed to our vacation home. After his death, I discovered that he'd put a second mortgage on this house. I can't pay for even one mortgage with my job as a waitress. And that doesn't count the money he owes Hal."

"Who's Hal?" I asked.

"Some bookie who's always texting him, even in the middle of the night," Angela explained. "He keeps making threats and wants to know when he's going to get his money. Jonas was distracted at his job, and the network was getting tired of him. Honestly? I think they were going to let him go when the season finished taping."

This was news to me. "But he was so popular. The public loved him."

"Sure they did," Angela remarked. "Because no one knew the real guy. He was a hell of an actor, with an award-winning smile. The director of *Senior Moments* was fed up with him."

"Corey?" Josie asked.

Angela nodded. "Sometimes Jonas didn't show up for tapings and threw everyone's schedule off. Then the station would call here to look for him. I kept telling them that Jonas didn't live here anymore, but they kept calling anyway. Now, I'm stuck with a mountain of bills and I have to plan a funeral."

"Isn't Jonas's family taking care of it?" I asked.

She gave a loud snort. "There's only his brother, and the poor schmuck is in a wheelchair. As usual, I get stuck doing everything. I just hope that the insurance policy comes through soon."

We have a winner. So, Angela was the beneficiary. It seemed impolite to ask how much she was inheriting, although I was dying to know. "Insurance policy? Did Jonas have any enemies? Was there someone who wanted him dead?" *Besides you, of course.*

She looked amused by the question. "Are you kidding? Most of the people he worked with couldn't stand him. He thought he was better than everyone because he was a celebrity."

"You seem to be taking his death well." Sarcasm dripped from Josie's mouth.

Angela shrugged. "Like I said, I loved him once, but that was a long time ago. He never ran around on me or physically abused me, but in my opinion, the addiction was just as bad. And now he's gone, and I can't change things. As my grandmother used to say, there's no use in crying over spilled milk."

The comment almost made me smile, but I caught myself in time. Grandma Rosa was famous for her mixed-up expressions, and that one was a particular favorite of hers. I'd grown up with her saying, "Don't cry over spilled sugar," which had never made sense to me.

"What makes you two think that you can find Jonas's killer before the police do?" Angela asked.

I hesitated before answering. If I told her about all the other murder investigations I'd been involved with, she might think that I was strange. Then again, she might be right. "The bakery is my livelihood. I have every faith in the police department, but they're quite overloaded at the moment. Every day that the bakery stays closed costs me a lot of money."

She nodded in understanding. "Well, good luck. You're going to need it."

"Where did Jonas go to play poker?" I asked.

Angela finished off her drink. "When he was in town, he'd play at the local casino, Let it Ride, on Saturday nights. They have a private poker room. When Jonas was on location with *Senior Moments*, he'd go in search of a new place. I tell you, the man could never get enough. He was drawn to it, like a drug user to crack. The signs were all there when we got married, but I chose to ignore them." She bit into her lower lip. "God, I was such a fool."

"Do you have any children?" Smiley had mentioned that he didn't have kids, but I wanted to gauge her reaction anyway.

"No, thank God. I wouldn't want to subject them to this crap." Angela rose from her chair. "Sorry, but I really do need to leave."

We followed her to the front door. I glanced over at Jake, still sleeping in his bed. He opened one eye, and I swore that he winked at me.

"Thanks for your time," Josie remarked.

"Yes, we appreciate it." I stepped onto the porch with Josie. "We're sorry for your loss and all that you've been through."

Angela blinked, and I thought I spotted an unshed tear in her eye. "It's all my own fault. I never should have gotten mixed up with him. Oh, well. At least the life insurance policy will help."

"I hope it's a substantial sum." I waited to see if she'd take the bait.

"Yeah, it's a cool million. Well, see you around." Before we could respond, Angela closed the door, missing my face by a mere inch. Josie and I stood there speechless for several seconds. With no other alternative, we turned and walked back to her minivan.

"Did we say something to tick her off?" I asked. "She seemed fine until the end."

"Maybe she thinks you figured out her motive," Josie suggested as we sped away. "Angela could have done away with him for the insurance money."

"We can't jump to conclusions yet," I said. "There's no proof. We're not even sure if she was in Colwestern the night that Smiley was murdered."

"The police must know by now." Josie stopped for a red light. "Or if she has an alibi. What do you want to do now? Head home?"

I glanced at the clock on the dashboard. Three thirty. "Are you in any rush to get home?"

Josie shook her head. "Rob took the kids out to lunch and then a movie. What'd you have in mind? Oh, wait. You want to go to Let it Ride, don't you?"

"Why not? The bakery is still closed, and Grandma said she'd keep Cookie for as long as I need her to. We may not get another chance to come back out this way."

"All right," Josie conceded. "Let me call Rob and tell him not to expect me until later tonight. I'm starving. We'll grab an early dinner and then head over. But what are we going to do for money? I know nothing about poker, and that place is probably high stakes. We can't afford to get into a game."

She was right. I contemplated this in silence for several seconds. "Maybe we could get inside the room somehow and watch what's going on."

"Yeah, right," Josie laughed. "It's not a spectator sport, Sal. I don't think they allow people in there to watch. Maybe you could pull off a Maria Muccio and get a temporary job as a cocktail waitress."

The reference made me smile. A couple of years ago, we'd taken a trip to Las Vegas to talk to a person of interest in the murder of Mrs. Gavelli's friend. During the process, we had stumbled across my father and mother at a local casino. Dad had been stalking a literary agent at the time, and my mother, anxious to do her part, had taken a job as a cocktail waitress at the agent's table.

Josie and I stopped at a nearby restaurant for an early dinner. When we finished, it was five o'clock. I left a message on Mike's voicemail to let him know I'd be home late. For the first time, I was actually relieved that he hadn't answered. Mike would not be happy about my late return and immediately suspect that it had more to do with Smiley's murder.

"Cookie is fine," Grandma Rosa assured me when I

called. "We are getting ready to have dinner with your parents." She held the phone to Cookie's ear. "Tell Mama what you are having for dinner."

"Sghetti!" Cookie shouted. "Bye. Ma!"

"Bye, baby. Love you." She was starting to talk so well. "They grow up fast," I said wistfully.

Josie laughed as she started the engine. "Tell me about it. Can you believe that Danny is in high school now? He's already talking about college. Sal, I'm not ready for my baby to leave home. And the cost is another thing that scares me."

"Another good reason why we have to make sure nothing affects our business," I said.

Let it Ride Casino was an impressive-sized building that included a hotel as well as a golf course for those who might not want to throw their money away. We left the minivan in a parking garage that adjoined the building. When we entered the casino through the glass doors, a rush of cigarette smoke greeted us, leaving me nauseated. "Maybe this wasn't such a good idea. The smoke is going to bother me."

"Yeah, it smells like an ash tray in here," Josie observed. "Come on, let's see if we can find the poker room."

We asked a cashier in one of the cages for directions. She pointed to the back of the casino, where an attendant was standing in front of a closed door. The man had shoulders on him that were as broad as a linebacker with a nametag that identified him as Dave. He raised one eyebrow as we approached.

"Need some help, ladies?" he asked. "Can't find the penny slots?"

"Hey…" Josie frowned. "We could play the dollar machines if we wanted to."

Good grief. "Uh, we were wondering if we could watch the poker games going on inside."

He shook his head. "Sorry, only players and employees are allowed inside."

"But how will I learn to play if I can't watch?" Josie asked.

Dave nodded to a bank of slot machines on his left. "Start with the poker slots. You won't lose as much money that way. They're much safer."

Josie produced a twenty from her purse and waved it in under his nose. "Are you sure there isn't any way we could get you to change your mind?"

Dave's mouth tightened. "Are you trying to bribe me, ma'am? If so, you could be in serious trouble."

"Oh, no, of course not!" Josie said quickly. "I, um, just decided that I'd like to play those penny slots after all. Where did you say they were?"

Dave almost smiled as he pointed to his left. "You'll find some in that area."

"Thank you." Josie flashed him a megawatt grin, but Dave was not easily fooled. We began to walk toward the slots. I took a chance and looked back over my shoulder at him. Dave's eyes were still fixated on our retreating figures.

"Gee, that was a great idea," I said as she sat down in front of a Deuces Wild poker machine. "Why didn't you let me ask him some questions first? He must know Smiley."

Before Josie could reply, someone grabbed my arm. Panicked, I whirled around and braced myself, ready to be escorted out the door by Dave. But Dave was nowhere to be seen. A pair of greenish-gold eyes gazed into mine with an expression of anger and disbelief.

"What in God's name are you two doing here?" Brian barked out.

CHAPTER NINE

"Okay, Sal, I'm going to let you take this one," Josie mumbled.

Brian's face was a shade of crimson as he brought it close to mine. "Sally, I'll ask you one more time. What are you ladies doing here?"

"It's a free country. We're simply having a girls' night out," I lied.

Brian moved back a step and studied my expression. "You're not a very good liar. Come on, let's have the truth. Like I don't already know what it is."

The jig was up. Defeated, I slumped into a seat by Josie. "All right. We're looking into Smiley's murder."

Brian kept his gaze pinned on me for so long that it started to get unnerving. Finally, I couldn't stand it any longer. "Aren't you going to say something?"

His lips moved slightly, and then I realized he was counting. "I'm trying very hard not to lose my temper."

"You're not doing so well," Josie observed.

Brian glowered at her then turned back to me. "What is it about me that you find so incompetent? Please. I'd really like to know why you feel that you can do my job better than I can."

Heat rose through my face. "Brian, this has nothing to do with you. I happen to think that you're a very good cop—detective, I mean."

His nostrils flared. "Sorry, Sally. We've been down this road too many times before, and I'm not buying it. So, tell me, what's the real reason? Or do you just enjoy showing me up?"

"Listen to me!" I shouted. A lady at a nearby *Wheel of Fortune* machine stared over at me in surprise, but thankfully no one else had heard me over the noise of the machines. "I can't just sit around and wait. I know the police department is overloaded.

Every day that my bakery has to stay closed is costing me money. Plus, I have a new house to pay for."

"And college," Josie added quickly. "I have to think about my kids' education. By the way, it's never too soon for you to start thinking about your son's future, Brian."

"Thanks for the tip." Brian's tone was tinged with sarcasm. "Actually, I was just about to call you. The investigation at your bakery is complete. You can reopen the place on Monday. Now that we have that settled, will you please go home?"

"There's more," I remarked. "Jerry Maroon sabotaged my bakery. Did you see the article in today's paper?"

A muscle twitched in Brian's jaw. "Yeah, I saw it. He'll never change. You must know that by now."

"Can't you and your coworkers stop that jerk from hanging around the police station?" Josie asked.

"There is such a thing as freedom of the press," Brian reminded her. "Believe me, I wish I could send Jerry on a one-way plane ride to Antarctica. You'd think he would have changed his ways after almost getting killed for playing roving reporter. Some people don't learn, I guess."

I wondered if his words were meant for me as well but decided not to ask. "The bakery isn't the only reason I'm checking into Smiley's death. If the killer isn't found within a certain amount of time, Nicoletta and my grandmother lose out on their trip to Italy."

For the first time tonight, the corners of Brian's mouth lifted into a small smile. "Okay, I get it now. Who wouldn't want to get rid of Nicoletta for ten days?"

"Darn straight," Josie agreed.

There was much more to it than Mrs. Gavelli, but I didn't bother to explain. Personally, I was more concerned with my grandmother going to Italy. Although she hadn't said anything, I suspected that she had some unfinished business there.

"What I want to know," Brian continued, "is how you learned that Smiley was associated with Let it Ride Casino. Time to come clean. Who told you about Smiley's gambling problem?"

There was no point in lying to him. "We stopped to talk to Angela Jones. She gave us all the details on their dysfunctional marriage and Smiley's addiction."

Brian muttered a curse word under his breath. "Why am I not surprised?"

"This is nothing against you," I said. "We only want to try and help things along."

Brian let out a breath that sounded like he'd been holding it for a week. "Look, I spoke with Angela yesterday and got all these details. I also talked to Smiley's brother James. He lives in Arizona and hasn't seen Smiley in a few months. They were close and talked at least a couple of times a week."

"Could he be a suspect in the murder?" I asked.

"Not a chance," Brian said. "James has an airtight alibi for the day Smiley was killed. He was devastated by his brother's death and thought the world of him. I guess Smiley helped him out of some financial jams in the past."

"That can't be right," Josie said. "Angela told us that they were having money problems due to his gambling. It's the reason she left him."

"Yes, she told me that too," Brian agreed. "But Smiley still helped James out whenever he had an extra dollar to his name. I mean, he had to win at poker once in a while, right? James has a lot of medical problems, so Smiley helped out with expenses—until recently. James said his brother pretty much had his paycheck spent before he received it. Sounds like the guy was in way over his head. James also said that Smiley has a large life insurance policy and he's the beneficiary."

Josie rose from her seat. "Well, someone forgot to tell Angela. She said that she's getting the money."

"It's very possible one of them could have killed Smiley for the money," I said. "If James wasn't here, maybe he hired someone to do the job for him."

Brian didn't look convinced. "That's a little far-fetched. Angela is definitely a suspect, but James is in a wheelchair, and I don't believe he's involved. We're not looking at him as a potential killer. I'm trying to find out who the beneficiary is, but the insurance company's not obligated to tell us. Smiley's will won't be read until it goes to probate."

"I don't know why Angela would lie about it," I said.

"What are you doing here, then?" Josie wanted to know.

He almost smiled. "The same as you, but it happens that I have a plan."

"Anything we can do to help?" I half expected Brian to burst out laughing and tell us to leave before he placed us under arrest.

His reply was slow in coming. "Look, I'm probably going to hate myself for saying this, but a couple of eavesdroppers like yourselves might come in handy tonight. And you're one of the best ones around, Sally."

I wasn't sure if I should take that as a compliment or an insult. Never mind. It was better not to know. "What do you want us to do?"

Brian pinned me with his bright green gaze. "I need your help tonight."

"I must be going deaf," I said. "I thought I heard you say that you needed my help with something."

"Did the earth just move under my feet?" Josie teased.

Brian ignored her comment. "Well, what do you say? Are you both up to it? I can promise you won't be in any danger."

"That's not what I was worried about. Only, I can't believe you're serious," I murmured.

"Yeah. I can't believe it either," Brian admitted. "I'm working this assignment alone tonight, and a couple of attentive listeners would be a huge help. With everyone's workload, no one was available to come with me tonight. Beggars can't afford to be choosers."

"Gee, thanks a lot." I couldn't help myself.

He looked sheepish. "Sorry. I didn't mean it the way it sounded. But I don't have the strength to keep fighting you every time there's a murder in our town. I'm getting too old for this."

"Oh please. You're only thirty-five," I scoffed.

"I've aged significantly since I met you," he said.

Another shot at my expense. "So, what exactly do you want us to do?"

Brian moved closer to me and glanced around the room. No one was paying any attention to us. "I've arranged with the manager to go undercover in the poker room to mingle with some of the players. But the area is large, and I can't cover it all by myself. There's room for an extra player but at a different table. What's it going to be? Do either one of you have any poker experience?"

"My father taught me how to play when I was a kid," I explained. "Back then, our entire family used to have a game every Saturday evening, but we only played for nickels and dimes. I can't afford to be in one of those games. I'm guessing the stakes are a little higher than nickels and dimes."

"It's nothing for you to worry about," Brian assured me. "I talked with the manager, and they'll spot you some chips. But you have to return whatever you have left at the end of the evening, whether you win or lose. Is that understood?"

"Sure, that's fine." It would certainly take the pressure off if I didn't have to use my own money, and I'd be able to enjoy the game more.

Brian cocked his head to the side and studied me. "Tell me the truth, Sally. If you don't know enough about the game, say so now. I can't have my cover blown."

"I am telling you the truth," I said. "Do you want me to recite the rules of the game? Three of a kind beats one pair, a straight beats three of a kind, a flush beats a straight, a full house beats—"

Brian held up his hand. "Okay, okay, I get it."

"Couldn't Sal and I play together at the same table?" Josie asked.

"Forget it," Brian said. "That's not about to happen. The two of you together would be a disaster. It would be like having Lucy and Ethel at the same table."

Josie tossed her head. "There's no need to be insulting."

"Where will I be?" I asked Brian.

Brian led us to a room marked *Employees Only*. "You and I need to be at separate tables so we can hear more of the conversation going on. With Smiley's recent death, it's highly possible that some of the players will be talking about him."

"Shouldn't I be dressed up more?"

Brian glanced down at my tunic shirt and shorts. "What you're wearing is fine. You'll blend right in. I don't expect that people will be dressed up."

"But everyone will be smoking." The idea of a claustrophobic room that reeked of cigarettes started the nausea going in my stomach again.

"Probably. Look, Sally, I'm not going to force you into this. It would help to have a couple of extra set of ears in there, but if you're not feeling well, I completely understand." He studied my face. "The question is, how badly do you want to find Smiley's killer?"

I blew out a long sigh. "All right. I'll do it."

"What about me?" Josie asked. "I don't know how to play poker. That's why I asked if Sal and I could be at the same table, so she could help teach me."

Brian opened a closet that was labeled *Uniforms* and gestured at two black minidresses hanging there. "The manager told me I could use anything that I needed to in here. These are the cocktail dresses that the server's wear."

Josie wrinkled her nose. "You've got to be kidding. Jeez, what am I? Sal's mom?"

He looked confused. "Did your mother work as a waitress, Sally?"

"No. It's a long story." I didn't want to discuss my mother's escapades right now. Brian thought my family was weird enough. "Well, what do you say, Jos?"

"All right," she agreed. "As long as the outfit isn't too revealing."

Brian shook his head. "The skirt is short, but the rest of the outfit is respectable enough. This isn't the Playboy bunny club." He took the dress off the rack and handed it to her.

Josie held it up against her and made a face. The dress looked as if it had been designed for someone of my five-foot-three-inch height. Josie was four inches taller than me.

"This is barely going to cover my butt," she complained. "Aren't there any other sizes or lengths available?"

"I'm afraid not." Brian shook his head and pointed at her sneakers. "You'll need to lose those too."

"Fine." Josie growled. "I have a pair of heels out in the van. They belong to one of my sisters, but at least we're the same size."

There was a small locker room for employees to change. Fortunately, it was vacant. "When you're ready, Sally, come into the poker room and sit at table four," Brian said. "Do not give any kind of indication that you know me. Don't even look my way. You can flirt and chat it up with your other tablemates. Josie, you need to flirt a *lot*. That's how cocktail waitresses make good tips. And no questions, just listen. Understand?"

"Jeez, Brian, give us a little credit," I said. "This isn't our first rodeo."

Brian shot me a dubious look. "Maybe not, but if we aren't careful, it could turn into one deadly stampede."

CHAPTER TEN

A half hour later, I found myself sitting at a table in the private poker room. Five people were in my group—one woman who looked to be in her late fifties and three men whose ages ranged from thirty to sixty. Small talk was made as cards were dealt. No one spoke to me except for the dealer, who politely asked if I wanted to stay in the pot. Almost everyone in the room was smoking, and my eyes immediately began to water. Good grief. Was there some kind of prerequisite that you had to be a smoker to enter the casino?

The colors and values of the chips were difficult to keep straight, so I had to keep consulting the cheat sheet Brian had given me. It was inside my purse, since I didn't want my tablemates to know this was my first time in the big leagues. Every few minutes I pretended to reach in my purse for another breath mint and would steal a glance at it. Green chips were worth twenty-five dollars, and everyone had to ante up one for each round. Our table was playing seven-card stud.

Okay, Sal. Focus. You can do this.

My eyes kept wandering around the room, trying to take in every possible sight and sound. Our dealer, Russ, a dark-haired man in his thirties, did various tricks with the cards as he shuffled and handed them out. Brian was to my right, a few feet separating our tables. He was smoking a pipe and chatting with an elderly man sitting next to him. Brian's table was playing Texas Hold'Em. He hadn't glanced my way once, which was probably a good thing, as discretion was not my friend today.

Josie was serving Brian's table drinks, looking confused and harassed at the same time. At least the cocktail dress showed off her figure to its best advantage. She didn't have black hose to go with it, but her legs were slim and tan, accentuated by the high heels. My mother would have been proud. A man with thick sideburns and shoulder-length black hair was eyeing Josie like she was dinner. *Gross.*

Russ started a new game, placing two cards down for each of us and then the next card up. "And it's a deuce, a lady for the lady, a king, and another deuce," he sang out as he went around the table.

After the third card had been dealt, the man seated next to me threw in a black chip. Time to take stock. Was that worth a hundred or five hundred dollars? Shoot, I couldn't remember. He turned to me expectantly, and I tossed a chip into the center of the table.

The woman flipped her cards facedown and pushed them to the side. "I fold."

A man at my left threw in a red chip and winked at me. "You're new here, aren't you?"

I tried to act casual. "It's not my first rodeo."

He looked confused. "Say what?"

"Never mind," I said hastily. "No, I've been here several times."

"Ma'am," Russ addressed me. "Are you in or out?"

I studied my cards. I had a queen of spades showing on the table with a seven and another queen in the hole with a deuce. I slid a white chip into the center of the table, and the man to my left laughed.

"Honey, stop the kidding around."

Crap. I'd already gotten the values mixed up. My family had never played with chips. If there was no money, we'd use candy. One time, when everyone was broke but still wanted to play, we'd used penne. It had worked well for the purpose.

I reached into my purse for my fourth breath mint while everyone waited impatiently. Finally, I threw a red chip in the center of the table.

"I haven't seen you in here before." The man to my right spoke in a low, husky voice as I collected my next card, another deuce. "You must come on Mondays. That's pool hall night for me, and I would remember a looker like you."

"Yes, that's right." I watched as he threw in a blue chip, and followed suit. "Mondays."

"It's nice to have someone attractive at our table for once." He grinned, displaying a huge gap between his yellow, stained front teeth. "By the way, I'm Tiny."

"Nice to meet you." I turned back to my cards, thinking that there wasn't anything tiny about the man. He had to be six feet tall and well over three hundred pounds. The name must be a joke.

My next card was a five of diamonds. "It's a terrible shame about what happened to the gentleman who played here."

"You mean Smiley?" Tiny asked.

"Yes, the gameshow host."

Brian's eyes shifted over to me at that moment, then quickly turned away. Whoops, he'd said not to ask questions. Oh well, too late now.

"They say he was murdered," I remarked.

The woman at my table clucked her tongue against the roof of her mouth. "Tragic. I heard that he was beaten to a pulp. Smiley was a nice man."

"Did you know him well?" I asked.

"Lucy, where's your bet?" This came from a balding man who had a rose tattoo on his forearm with Stella written on it.

Lucy glared at him and immediately folded. Tiny, tattoo man, and I were the only ones left.

"It was only a matter of time." Tiny threw a purple chip into the pot.

I checked my cheat sheet and almost gasped out loud. Purple was worth five hundred dollars.

Tattoo guy was deep in thought, debating about what to do. Finally, he also threw in a purple chip. I had a sole one in my possession. Panicked, I tried to calculate the amount in the center of the table and failed miserably. A thousand? No, it was more like three thousand. My hands started to shake, even though this wasn't my money. How could these people throw away so much cash at the drop of a hat? I was lucky if my bakery did that much dough in one week.

Oh, what the heck. You only live once, right? I tossed the purple chip in.

"Go get him, honey," Lucy murmured as she lit up a cigarette.

Tiny had a pair of Kings showing, plus a deuce and a five. He turned over the other three cards to reveal an eight, another five, and two deuces. Tattoo man muttered a curse word under his breath. He had a straight, ten high. They both watched as I revealed my cards, and a low murmur went around the table.

"Full house," I said proudly. "Queens over fives."

"Go ahead. Take it, doll," Tiny said. "I'll get even next time."

I spread out my arms and swept the chips toward me in excitement. At that particular moment, I thought I understood how a person might become a gambling addict. It was such a rush—a complete feeling of euphoria that you were on top of the world.

"How'd you know Smiley if you came here on Mondays?" Tiny asked. "He only played here on Saturdays."

"Yeah, he was our Saturday Night Fever guy," tattoo guy remarked.

Everyone at our table laughed except for Lucy.

"You guys are awful," she hissed. "The poor man was beaten to death with a rolling pin. It's tragic!"

"Oh, my goodness," I gasped. "I had no idea that was how he died."

"Ante up. Seven-card stud," Russ announced.

Everyone tossed a green chip into the center of the table.

As I'd hoped, Lucy continued where she'd left off. "Sad to say, but it was only a matter of time for the poor guy. Hal would have made mincemeat out of him eventually."

"Who's Hal?" I asked.

"Come on, doll," Tiny said impatiently. "Place your bet. I'm getting' old here."

His comment drew another round of laughter as Josie approached our table. She placed a glass of beer next to Tiny, who gave her an appreciative look. "Thanks, beautiful. Hey, what time do you get off work?"

"Never," Josie spat out, obviously forgetting that she was supposed to be gracious to the players.

I shut my eyes, sensing disaster was about to strike. I should have phoned my mother to fill in. She would have gladly made the trip out here, but that would have meant my father coming along, too. Dad would have gotten himself thrown out of the room after asking everyone what their casket preferences were.

"Jeez, she's a cold one," Tiny muttered as Josie left the room to get tattoo guy a gin and tonic.

"What about Hal?" I asked Lucy. "Was he a friend of Smiley's?"

Everyone laughed as Lucy shook her head. "Let's just say that Hal Derby is a friend to those who need dough," she explained. "And Smiley was into Hal for a lot of dough. Maybe Hal decided it was time to collect."

"You mean a bookie?"

My question had been innocent enough, but everyone looked at me as if I'd said an obscene word.

"Maybe Stan did it," Tiny joked and pointed at tattoo guy. "Smiley took him to the cleaners the last time he was here."

Stan's face turned as red as a tomato. He immediately rose to his feet, knocking his chair over in the process. "I never touched the guy! What's your problem, Tiny?"

Tiny raised his hands in the air. "Hey, man. I don't have a problem. I'm just telling it like it is."

"Why, you filthy piece of—" Stan took a step forward, and instinctively I flinched. Great. A brawl in a poker room? I hadn't signed on for this. I glanced over at Brian, who was still mulling over his cards.

"Come on, guys, settle down." Russ spoke in a warning tone. "I don't want to have to get Security in here."

Stan looked over at Tiny, then sat back down and picked up his cards. "I don't want to talk about that joker anymore. He got what was coming to him."

Lucy's eyes grew round like sugar cookies as she tossed a yellow chip into the pot. "That's a horrible thing to say."

"The guy owed money to everyone and their mother," Stan said matter-of-factly. "A true addict. You want to know what I think? His addiction was the death of him."

"Honey, what the heck are you doing?" Tiny asked. "We're all waiting on you. Better stop daydreaming."

"Sorry." I tossed a chip into the pot.

Russ rolled his eyes at me. "Please make the appropriate bet, ma'am."

Holding my breath, I threw in a yellow chip.

"It ain't her first rodeo," Stan snickered.

So much for my attempts to fly under the radar.

Lucy tapped her ace of spades showing on the table. "I'm betting that the director on his show did it. He's no good."

Okay, now we were getting somewhere.

Tiny lit a cigarette and blew a circle of smoke in my direction as I desperately tried not to gag. "Why do you think that?" I asked.

"Because I took Smiley out for breakfast one morning after the game wound down," she said. "He'd lost his shirt, and I felt kind of bad for the guy. Smiley got to talking about the show and said that he thought the director might try to get him canned. Seems like the director was fooling around with the makeup girl. The director's wife would be none too happy if she found that out."

My ears pricked up. Corey was a possible suspect, too? I wanted to take a minute to process all of this new information, but Stan interrupted my train of thought.

"Hey." He rapped on the table. "Get with the program, please. I ain't got all night."

"Sure, you do," Tiny snickered. "You're always the last one to leave."

"Sorry." I reached for the card being dealt before I realized that it was Tiny's.

He emitted a growl low in this throat. "Try to keep up, okay?"

Heat rose through my face. "Oh! I'm so sorry!"

Tiny lifted his cards and frowned. "If I wanted to play with kids, I would have stayed in high school."

"You probably flunked out anyway," Lucy chimed in.

There was another round of laughter, but Tiny didn't look amused. I wondered how much longer I could keep this up. In desperation, I looked over at Brian again. He was talking to a woman with red dyed hair seated on his right. When he turned his head, our gazes met, and I frantically tried to send him a message with my eyes. *When. Can. I. Leave.* He stared at me with a blank expression and then turned his attention back to his cards. *Gee, thanks a lot.*

At that moment, Josie re-entered the room with a tray of drinks between her hands. Tiny pushed his chair back, not realizing she was behind him, and all I could do was watch, mesmerized, as Josie and the tray went flying through the air. Liquor and glasses crashed to the floor, with everyone at the tables jumping to their feet and talking all at once. Forgetting my cards, I hurried over to help her up. I stole a sideways glance at Brian, who was no longer gazing at his cards. He was staring up at the ceiling with eyes closed, while his lips formed one lone curse word.

"Are you all right?" Tiny asked.

"Why don't you watch where you're going!" Josie said angrily.

"Jeez, honey, it was an accident. I'm sorry," Tiny began.

Josie was on a roll now. "And don't call me honey!" she screamed. "This job bites. I'm outta here." She turned on her stiletto heel, wobbling slightly to one side. Fortunately, I caught her in time. Josie couldn't pull off heels like my mother. Heck, no one could.

"Be careful, miss." I looked around at everyone gawking. "The poor thing's so upset that she almost tripped."

"Everything okay in here?" A security guard had appeared from out of nowhere.

Josie left the tray on the floor and flounced out of the room without so much as a backward glance at me. I started to pick the tray up then caught Brian's eye. Bad move. I moved back to my seat and picked up my cards. "Such a shame," I said to Lucy. "She told me it's her first week on the job."

Stan whispered something to Lucy, and they both eyed me sharply but said nothing further. Heat rose in my face. I had a feeling the jig was up for me as well but didn't dare leave until I got some kind of sign from Brian.

A new man had entered the poker room during the commotion and was seated at the table directly in front of mine. He had his back to me, but there was something strangely familiar about him. I stared at the back of his head, trying to figure it out. He wore a Mets ballcap over his short dark hair and sat hunched over, ready to collect his cards. *Come on, turn around, mister.*

"Yo, lady? You in or what?" Stan asked impatiently.

A blonde waitress entered the room, and the new player gestured at her. She went over and took his drink order.

"Earth to rodeo girl!" Stan shouted.

I blinked several times and quickly threw in a chip. "Sorry, I guess I was somewhere else."

"Yeah, well, I'm starting to wish that you *were* somewhere else," Stan snapped. "We're here to play poker, lady, not people watch."

Stan's remark barely registered with me since I was still consumed with the identity of the new player. Where had I seen this man before? He said something to the dealer then cocked his head to the right, which allowed me to glimpse his profile. My heart stuttered in my chest when recognition set in.

It was Slim Daniels.

CHAPTER ELEVEN

"Ma'am? It's your bet," Russ told me.

I was so distracted by Slim's appearance that I couldn't reply.

"Hey, lady, are you with us or not?" Stan wrapped his knuckles loudly on the table, startling me out of my stupor. One of the cards flew out of my hand and onto the floor. Sheepishly, I glanced around at my tablemates. From my their annoyed expressions, it was obvious they were losing patience with me.

"Get a move on." Stan barked. He handed me back the ace that I'd literally thrown away. "You're breaking my concentration. What's your problem?"

"Sorry," I mumbled. "Suddenly, I have the most horrible migraine."

Lucy gave me a sympathetic look. "Oh, those are the worst." She took another puff of her cigarette, blowing smoke in my direction.

"Gee, I don't know what could have brought it on," I gagged.

Lucy didn't get the joke. She held up her glass of beer. "There's only one cure for that. Drink lots of liquids."

Everyone but Stan laughed.

My mind was racing with ideas. What was Slim doing here? He obviously knew Smiley beyond the game show. "I probably should take a break," I said.

"What?" Tiny asked in surprise.

"You don't quit until I get my money back," Stan yelled.

His outcry had started to attract the attention of the other tables. Slim turned around to see what the commotion was about, and our eyes met. An expression of disbelief replaced by panic crossed his face. He said something to the dealer, scooped up his chips, and quickly left the table.

I threw my cards down, attempting to follow him, but Stan caught my arm as I tried to pass.

"Let go of me!" I shrieked.

He released his grip on my arm. "What do you think you're doing?"

"Oh, right. Sorry." I turned around, hastily swept the chips into my purse, and took off in hot pursuit. I was vaguely aware of Brian's amazed look as I ran by, but there was no time to explain. As I ran through the casino, I managed to pull out my phone and pressed the button for Josie's name.

"What?" she asked irritably.

I almost ran into an elderly woman with a walker next to a slot machine. "Sorry," I called as I flew by. "Jos, where are you? Slim is here, and I need your help before he leaves the building!"

"Oh, my God! I'm in the van. I'll be right there." She clicked off.

Slim tore by another bank of penny slots. It looked as if he was headed for the exit. I quickened my pace to catch up with him but had to stop abruptly when two waitresses stepped in front of me with trays full of drinks. By the time they had moved aside, Slim was nowhere to be seen.

Unsure of what else to do, I raced out the entrance anyway, hoping for a glimpse of him. The sun had sunk a while ago, but the building was awash in light. A Security guard was over by the valet parking sign, talking on his phone. He looked up as I hurried over to him,

"Excuse me! Did you see a man just run by here? A tall, skinny guy, wearing a Mets ball cap."

The attendant shook his head. "No ma'am. Is everything okay? Do I need to call the police?"

"That won't be necessary," a cool male voice said behind me.

Uh-oh. I closed my eyes and waited several seconds before turning around to meet Brian's annoyed gaze. Panicked, I began to babble. "Look, I can explain."

The attendant was staring at both of us in confusion. Brian gave him a gleaming smile and guided me with his elbow. "Come along, dear."

When we were far enough away from the attendant, Brian released my arm. He squared his shoulders and placed his hands on his slim hips. "Why did you get up and leave like that? Josie's a big girl. You didn't need to run to her aid. And you ruined my chance to find out about Smiley!"

"I didn't leave because of Josie," I said. "Slim Daniels was the guy who came in right after Josie dropped her tray. Didn't you recognize him?"

Brian's mouth fell open. "No, I must have missed him. What was he doing here?"

"That's what I'd like to know. As soon as he saw me, he bolted for the door. Slim must have known Smiley on a more personal level than we thought."

"Sally, I'm sorry," Brian said quietly. "Sounds like you were on top of your game tonight. Yes, pun intended."

"Wait a second. Are you actually giving me a compliment?" I handed him back my supply of poker chips.

His lips twisted into a smile. "Yes, but don't get used to it."

"Sal!" Josie ran towards us from the parking garage. "Did you get a chance to talk to him?"

"No. Slim got away, but he recognized me. I'm positive of that," I said. "That's why he got up and left the room."

"He must be hiding something," Josie said. "What's he doing in Rochester? Shouldn't he be working on another episode of *Senior Moments* by now?"

Brian drew a small pad out of his blazer pocket and thumbed through it. "During my talk with him the other day, Slim mentioned that he was only hired to help out with the Colwestern episode of *Senior Moments* because he's lives in Buffalo."

"Slim must be involved somehow," Josie declared. "What's he doing an hour away from Buffalo? There are casinos closer to his house that he could go to."

"Do you have his address?" I asked Brian. "Let's go to his house."

"Whoa." Brian raised his hand in the air. "I think you two have done enough for the night. Helping in the casino is one thing, but your involvement ends here."

Josie's jaw dropped. "Oh, come on. Can't we—"

Brian folded his arms across his chest. As far as he was concerned, the subject was closed. "Did either of you find out anything about Smiley?"

I leaned against the brick wall of the building, feeling

dizzy after my marathon sprint. "The players at my table all knew him. They said that Smiley owed a lot of money to a man named Hal Derby. I'm guessing he's a bookie, but they didn't seem to want to elaborate."

Brian studied the pad again. "Derby? Yeah, he's got an office here."

"What?" Josie asked in surprise. "How is that possible?"

"Bookies can do business in conjunction with the casino," Brian explained. "I can try to talk to him, but I've got to find him first. And that's not always an easy thing to do with bookies. They usually disappear into thin air when they know a cop is around."

I placed a hand over my mouth. "Oh my gosh, I almost forgot something! Smiley told Lucy—the woman at my table—that Corey Whitaker is married and having an affair with the makeup girl."

"There you go," Josie said. "Another suspect for you, Detective. Corey might have been afraid Smiley would reveal his dirty little secret."

Brian made another note on his pad. "Sally, you did well tonight. You definitely found out a lot more than I did."

"What about me?" Josie asked.

"You?" Brian's mouth turned up at the corners. "Stick to baking. You and alcohol don't mix well."

Josie sighed. "Yeah, you're right. Besides, my feet are killing me."

"Stilettos aren't for the faint of heart," I joked. "Just ask my mother."

* * *

It was almost eleven o'clock when I pulled into my driveway. The house was shadowed in darkness, illuminated by one lone lamp in the living room. Spike greeted me at the front door, wagging his tail in excitement. I gave him a hug, then went into the kitchen with him trailing after me.

I switched on the light and helped myself to a glass of iced tea from the fridge. My throat was still sore from all the secondhand smoke I'd inhaled, and the cold drink helped to soothe it. As I leaned against the counter, I took a minute to enjoy the stillness of the night and glanced around me with pleasure at the gleaming new kitchen. It was everything I'd dreamed of and more. Mike had built me a huge island in the center of the room, with a black and white marble countertop. Cookie's highchair was pulled up next to it, along with three other stools. There were so many glass cabinets hanging from the ceiling that I didn't know how I'd ever fill them all.

As much as I loved the kitchen, the family room was my favorite. The cathedral ceiling and crystal chandelier gave the room an air of sophistication, but it had a comfy feel at the same time. I could envision my family enjoying cozy evenings watching television or playing board games in front of the gas fireplace.

A winding oak staircase led to four spacious bedrooms upstairs. Two were still vacant, but I had high hopes they would be filled with children's furniture in the next few years. I needed to be patient. As Grandma Rosa said, "Good things come to those who wait."

I walked into the laundry room that adjoined the kitchen. Spike had already settled into his comfortable new bed on the floor. His food bowl and toys were in here as well. I noticed that his water bowl was empty as I stooped down to stroke his soft, furry head. "How do you like your new digs, fella?"

"What are you doing, Sal?"

Startled, I almost jumped ten feet in the air. I turned around to see Mike leaning against the wall, wearing nothing but a pair of blue plaid boxers. His black curly hair was a tousled mess. Midnight-blue eyes gazed inquisitively into mine, making my heart beat faster.

"Did I wake you?" I went over and kissed him.

He placed an arm around my shoulders, and we walked back into the kitchen together. "I don't sleep well when you're not here. It didn't help that I was worried, too."

"But I said that I'd be late. Josie and I went to Let it Ride Casino."

He made a face. "You smell like you smoked a pack of cigarettes."

I reached into the fridge for some more iced tea. "Don't worry, I'll take a shower before I come to bed."

Mike leaned against the island and ran a hand through his disheveled curly hair. "What the heck were you doing there? You don't gamble."

"No, but Smiley does—or did," I added.

Mike threw up his hands in disgust. "I knew it. Please tell me that no one tried to shoot at you tonight."

"Nope, nothing like that." I gulped down the rest of my drink. "Something is up, though. I saw one of the crew members from *Senior Moments* there. As soon as he spotted me, he took off."

"Great." Mike shook his head. "Does that mean he'll be coming after you? I thought you said that you were only going to talk to Smiley's wife."

"That was the original plan," I explained, "but when she told us that Smiley had a gambling problem, we went to check out the casino where he played. And then when Brian saw us there, he—"

Mike's eyes widened. "Brian was at the casino?"

There was a time when Mike had been jealous of Brian, although I'd never given him any reason to be. He knew Brian was interested in me when I'd returned to Colwestern five years ago. But Mike had been intent on winning me back and didn't let that stop him. He had come a long way since high school and the insecurities he'd suffered as a teenager. Brian and Mike would never be close friends, but they respected each other, and Mike appreciated Brian's work in law enforcement.

"Yes, he was there undercover. Smiley was a regular in the poker room. Brian asked if Josie and I would help him out for a while."

"Has the police department gone crazy?" Mike asked in disbelief. "What did you have to do?"

"I played poker for a while, but don't worry, I didn't lose any money. I asked a few questions about Smiley and even got some answers." I placed my glass in the sink and put my arms around his waist. "Brian has a new lead to check out after tonight, so it was worth it. You're worrying over nothing."

"I wish I could believe that." Mike sighed heavily. "But this is you that we're talking about."

I decided to change the subject. "How was Cookie tonight?"

"Great." He smiled. "Your grandmother sent us home with a cheesecake. As soon as I put some on a plate, Cookie tried to shove it all into her mouth at once."

"Let's face it. She's her mother's daughter. Look, I'm going to run into the bathroom down here to take a quick shower, and then I'll be up."

He blew me a kiss. "You'll be able to use the one upstairs tomorrow. The paint will have dried by then."

"Sounds good."

Mike winked. "I'll be waiting impatiently upstairs. Oh, there's a package and some envelopes that came in the mail for you today."

"Thanks. Maybe it's the curtains that I ordered for Cookie's room." I went into the laundry room to grab Spike's bowl, filled it in the sink, and placed it back on the floor. Afterwards, I ran into the small bathroom across the hall, stripped off my clothes, and jumped into the shower. Ten minutes later, I emerged, wrapped in a big fluffy pink towel with another one around my head.

I started for the stairs but, at the last second, remembered the mail on the kitchen table. In addition to the credit card bill, the curtains I'd been waiting for had arrived, along with a manila envelope. Absently, I checked for a return address in the left-hand corner. There was none. I flipped the envelope over to find a messy scrawl on the other side, and sucked in some air.

The envelope was from Smiley Jones.

CHAPTER TWELVE

My heart began to thump violently against the wall of my chest. I stared down at the envelope, thinking that there must be some mistake. I'd just received mail from the dead. What would Smiley have sent, and how had he even known where to find me?

Then I thought back to the last time I'd seen the man. Smiley had been holding a manila envelope—one similar to this—and behaving strangely. I had given him my address for an autographed picture. Had he known his life was in danger, and could the contents from the envelope somehow identify his murderer?

With trembling fingers, I opened the envelope, feeling like a presenter at the Academy Awards, dying to know the winner's name. *Oh, stop with the puns, Sal.* Disappointment spread through me as I examined the contents. Two playing cards. An ace of spades and the queen of spades. That was all.

Why the heck would Smiley be sending me playing cards instead of a photo in the mail?

"Princess, are you coming to bed?" Mike wanted to know.

The sound of his voice startled me. I hadn't even heard him come into the room. Mike was standing in the doorway, watching me, but his sexy smile faded when he saw my expression. "Sal, what is it? You look like you've seen a ghost."

"No, but I just received mail from one."

Mike lifted the ace of spades from the table. "What's this?"

"Smiley sent me these cards. He must have mailed them to me right before he died." I reached for my cell. "I have to let Brian know."

"At this hour?" Mike asked in surprise.

"I'll send a text. He's going to want to know about this

right away." I quickly typed out a message to him. *Just opened an envelope sent to me by Smiley, right before he died.*

A minute later, my cell buzzed. "Okay," Brian said. "Why would Smiley be sending you mail? I wasn't aware the two of you were that close."

"Remember what I told you about the conversation we had the night he died? Smiley looked unwell, and I offered him a cup of coffee. He was talking to me about cards." A light bulb switched on in my head. "Holy cow. It's the ace of spades that Officer Walden said was missing from the deck. Did Smiley know he was going to die? Was this some kind of cry for help?"

Brian snorted into the phone. "I think that's a bit dramatic. It's not like the mail was going to reach you five minutes later. Maybe he sent it to you because he knew he was in danger."

"But why me?" I asked.

He hesitated. "Like I said, Smiley may have known that his life was in danger. Or perhaps he'd heard about your reputation."

An icicle formed between my shoulder blades, and I shivered. "You're not making me feel any better about this."

"I'm sorry," Brian said. "But let's face the facts here, Sally. You're already in too deep with this investigation. Whether I like it or not, you're here to stay."

Sadly, I knew he was right. "Did you find Slim?"

"Not yet," Brian said. "I went to his house, but no one was home."

Perhaps Slim was staying away on purpose. "The television crew is still at a local hotel, right?"

"They're at the Hilton," Brian said. "It doesn't apply to Slim since he's local, and remember, he's not a permanent employee. As for the rest of the crew, including Corey, we've asked them to remain in town while we investigate further. Legally we can't hold them here much longer."

"Is the makeup woman staying there too? She's the one Corey is supposedly having an affair with."

"Yes, Tina is there, as well as half a dozen other crew members. Are you sure it's the makeup woman he's involved with? There was another woman on set. I have to check my notes for her name."

"Skye," I said.

"Yes, that's right. Skye Crandall. I interviewed her the night Smiley was killed."

I was trying to keep track of everyone involved in *Senior Moments* but failed miserably. "Is she local too?"

"Yes," Brian said. "Like Slim, she was only hired for the day. Unlike Slim, she's cooperating fully with the authorities. Everyone else has been good about it, except for Corey. He was very upset because they had to cancel an upcoming shoot. Do you think that Smiley could have been carrying on with Tina or Skye?"

"Personally, I doubt it. From what Angela said, Smiley was a little too preoccupied with his gambling addiction to give women a second thought. Skye seemed very young to me—young enough to still be in school."

"She recently celebrated her twenty-first birthday, while Tina's closer to thirty. Skye's a fashion design major at New York University and was able to land an internship through the network. She was on their call list if needed. Tina, on the other hand, has been with *Senior Moments* for over two years."

Corey was definitely involved with Tina, not Skye. I'd noticed some of the crew members watching her appreciatively the other day as she'd powdered Dodie's nose. "Are there any other women who work for *Senior Moments*?"

"There's a grip worker," Brian said, "That's a technician who operates the rigging and equipment that supports the camera. She didn't work on this location, though. I learned from the network's VP that she planned to join the crew for their next shoot."

Mike flipped the cards back and forth, obviously bored with my conversation.

I held up a finger to him and whispered, "Just one more minute."

"It might not hurt to try to speak with Tina at the hotel again," Brian said. "Since tomorrow's Sunday and the bakery is closed, would you like to come with me?"

I stared at the phone in amazement. Two times in the same day, Brian had asked for my help. This was a new record. "Are you sure that you're feeling okay?"

He gave a low chuckle. "Yeah, I know this doesn't sound like me, especially after everything I said earlier. Tina seemed very uncomfortable with me during the questioning, and Skye did, too. Most people are nervous when they're questioned by the police, even if they're innocent. I figured that if Tina had another woman to talk to instead of me, she might relax and reveal more information."

"All right. What time tomorrow?" I asked.

"Is ten o'clock good?" Brian wanted to know. "If that works, I'll pick you up at your house."

I hesitated and looked over at Mike. He rolled his eyes at the ceiling, obviously aware of what was happening. "Yes, I'll be ready." I clicked off.

"Let me guess," Mike groaned. "Brian wants you to do one more little favor for him."

"He only asked if I would go with him tomorrow when he questions the makeup artist from *Senior Moments*," I explained. "Brian seems to think that she'd be more receptive talking to a woman instead of him."

A muscle ticked in Mike's jaw. "When is this going to end, Sal? Or is it *ever* going to end?"

"Please don't be mad." My voice started to quiver. "I don't want to lose my business and the reputation that Josie and I have worked so hard to build."

Mike's shoulders sagged as he reached out and hugged me against him. "Yeah, I understand that. I don't like it, but I do understand. Look at this from my perspective, though. I worry that you're going to end up in danger again, and you usually do. No offense, but it's like there's a target on your back, and every killer who comes through New York State has a clear view of it." He tucked a stray curl behind my ear. "I need you, and Cookie needs her mother."

"You two will always come first in my life, but there is another reason I want to find Smiley's killer." I stuffed the playing cards back in the envelope and tossed the package into my purse. "The trip to Italy. Something's telling me that my grandmother has to go."

Mike's eyebrows drew together in confusion. "What are you saying? That something's going to happen to her?"

God forbid. My grandmother simply had to live forever. There was no way that any of us would ever survive without her. "I don't know exactly. It's just a feeling that I have."

He tweaked my nose playfully. "What about Nicoletta? Have you got a feeling about her too?"

"Irritation is the only thing that comes to mind when I think about her," I said with a laugh.

"Sad but true," Mike agreed.

"Honestly? It sounds terrible, but I'm not concerned whether Nicoletta goes or not. But my grandmother has to go."

"Don't worry, she will," Mike assured me. "We'll make it happen. I promise."

* * *

Brian arrived ten minutes early to pick me up the next morning, but I was ready. Cookie was busy playing with her toy radio on the living room floor, while Mike lay on the couch, watching the Sports Channel. I leaned down to kiss him. "I shouldn't be very long.

"Yeah, where have I heard that before?" He let out a yawn. "Maybe I'll set Cookie's baby swing up in the back yard while you're gone. She can help me. Isn't that right, baby?"

"Me!" Cookie shouted. "Kiss!"

I lifted her up in my arms and kissed her satin-like cheek. She tried to wiggle free, so I placed her on Mike's lap. "Say bye-bye to Mama," he told her."Bye Ma!" Cookie waved her hand furiously at me. She looked delighted that I was leaving, but I didn't take it personally. She loved spending time with her father.

I hurried out the door and got into the passenger side of Brian's sedan. He sped off before I had time to fasten my seat belt. "Jeez, what's the rush?"

He swiveled his head in my direction. "As of this morning, the TV crew was allowed to leave town. We can't hold them here any longer. But I'm hoping we can catch Tina before she takes off."

"Any news on Slim yet?"

He shook his head. "One of my officers checked his house again at about three o'clock this morning, but no one was home. I did find out something interesting about Smiley, though."

"Oh? What's that?"

Brian gripped the wheel tightly between his hands. "Off the record, I have a friend who works for the same life insurance company Smiley has his policy with. He did some checking around and told me that the life insurance policy was for a million dollars. It's still in Angela's name, not his brother's. Smiley never changed it. James has a rude awakening ahead of him."

"Yowza." I blew out a breath. "And he really needs the money, right?"

"Yes, but I've already told you he's not a suspect. Angela, on the other hand, goes to the top of my list. If the rumors you heard last night at the casino are true, Corey would have had a reason to get rid of Smiley as well."

"We still don't know what Slim's connection is either," I pointed out.

Brian pulled up in front of the Hilton. "There might not be a connection. He's allowed to go to poker rooms like anyone else."

"Sorry, but I'm not buying it," I said. "Buffalo has plenty of casinos around. There was no need for him to go all the way to Rochester. What did he say when you interviewed him the night Smiley died?"

"Not much," Brian pulled his car into the hotel's parking lot. "Slim said that he met Smiley on the day of the shooting. Apparently, he gets a lot of his work that way. It pays the bills, he told me."

We walked through the lobby and pressed the button for the elevator. Tina's room was located on the third floor. Brian knocked once. No answer. He waited a few seconds and knocked again. We heard someone unlock the door, then Tina peered out at us. She made a face when she recognized Brian and tried to slam the door in his face.

Brian wedged his foot into the opening. "Good morning, Miss Hoover. I was wondering if I could ask you a few more questions."

"I'm getting ready to leave," she said in annoyance. "We were told that we didn't have to stay here any longer. Everyone else has already gone." She stared over at me, and I spotted recognition in her eyes. "Hey, you're the one from the bakery. Why are you here?"

I smiled pleasantly. "Brian and I are—"

To my surprise, Brian placed an arm around my shoulders. "Sally's my wife. That's another reason why I have a personal interest in this case."

Tina looked confused. "But I thought that you were married to the hunky-looking guy who came into the bakery with the baby."

Jeez, Brian. Give a girl more of a warning next time. "Oh no. That was my brother," I explained quickly. "And the little girl is my niece."

She seemed placated by my response. "Oh. Well, I'm in a hurry, so get to the point."

"May we come in for a second?" I asked.

Tina blew out a sigh but pushed the door open to allow us entrance. Her suitcase and a backpack were sitting on top of the unmade bed. There was a dresser and a small table in the corner with two chairs. I sat in one, while Tina plopped down in the other. Brian's phone buzzed, and he read the screen.

"I need to take this." His mouth tightened, and I had a feeling that the call might have to do with Smiley's murder. "Sweetheart, can you keep Tina company for a few minutes until I'm all done?"

Oh brother. Well, if he could play this game, so could I. "Sure thing, lambchop."

Brian flicked a bewildered gaze my way. Once he regained his composure, he blew me a kiss and went into the hallway.

Tina fiddled with an empty beer can on the table. "Are you always in the habit of assisting your husband with his job?"

"No, but I have a personal interest in Smiley's death. It doesn't help your business when a game show host is beaten to death with one of your rolling pins."

"No, I guess not," she agreed. "Look, I hope you don't mind me saying this, but he's really hot."

I stuck my nose in the air and gave her a superior smile. "No worries. People tell me that all the time. Between you and me? I stole him away from another woman."

"Shut up." Tina's mouth dropped open. "Do you mean that he was married?"

"Yeah, but not happily." Good grief, the lies were pouring out of me like a fountain. "Everyone tried to warn me. 'Don't get involved with a married man, Sal. He'll cheat on you too. But it's not true.'"

Tina leaned forward in her chair. "Really? I'd like to believe that because—" She stopped suddenly and didn't finish the sentence.

"It's okay." I reached out and patted her hand. "Your secret is safe with me."

She stiffened and drew her hand away. "What secret?"

"About you and Corey, silly."

"You're crazy!" She shrieked and rose from the chair. "Who told you that lie? There's nothing going on between us."

"No one told me anything. I figured it out for myself. I've been there as well, so it was kind of obvious to me."

A trapped look came into Tina's blue eyes. "No," she insisted. "You're wrong."

I ignored her denial. "How long have you two been together?"

To my surprise, a tear dripped off her chin and fell onto the table, glistening under the bright ceiling light. "Nine months. He keeps telling me that he's going to leave his wife, but I…I just don't know. I'm starting to have doubts. How long were you two together before he broke it off with his wife?"

"A year." Guilt washed over me. I didn't like being deceptive. Tina was clearly being used by Corey, and I doubted he would leave his wife for her. "Does anyone else know?"

She sniffed loudly. "A couple of people. Smiley used to crack stupid jokes whenever he saw us talking on the set. It made Corey awfully mad."

"Men," I huffed. "They can be such jerks."

"For real," she agreed. "I told Corey that if he didn't break up with Janet soon, I was leaving. Do you know what he said? He told me that he'd make sure I never got a job with another TV station. Do you think he's using me?"

Thankfully, there was a tap on the door at that moment. "Oh, it must be my husband." I tried to sound more casual than I felt. "Why don't I tell Brian to go grab a coffee so you and I can talk some more. How's that sound?"

Tina blew her nose into a tissue. "It would be great, thanks. I could use someone to talk to right now."

"No problem." I rose and crossed the room to open the door, feeling cautiously optimistic. Tina seemed to have taken me into her confidence and I wondered what else I could find out. What would Corey have done to keep his tryst with Tina from reaching his wife's ears? He'd left my bakery about a half hour before Smiley departed, but could have returned without anyone knowing. Had he also been the one to steal my key ring?

All I needed was a few more minutes with Tina to see what else she'd reveal about her two-timing letch of a boyfriend.

Nothing would stop me now.

"Honey," I called out as I opened the door. "We need a few more minutes."

Only, it wasn't Brian at the door. I realized my mistake a second too late when I stared up into the bewildered and angry dark eyes of Corey Whitaker.

"What the heck are you doing here?" he snapped.

CHAPTER THIRTEEN

Once the initial shock wore off, I did my best to act casual. I could only hope that the panic I was experiencing on the inside was not displayed on my face.

"Corey, right? How are you?"

Corey looked different from the last time I'd seen him. His face had a haggard quality to it, as if he hadn't slept in days. At the moment, it was also turning a deep, unattractive shade of purple.

"Get out," he hissed. "I know all about you."

"Hey!" Tina rose from her chair and went to my side. "Don't be mean to her. She's really nice, even for a cop's wife."

Uh-oh. The dough was about to hit the fan.

Corey stared at his girlfriend like she had the word *stupid* tattooed on her forehead. "You've got to be kidding," he said. "She's not married to a cop. Didn't you read the article in the local paper about her the other day?"

I glanced at my watch and then moved past them towards the door. "Look at the time! I have to run. It was great seeing you again, Tina."

Corey reached out and grabbed my wrist in such a tight grip that I almost wept. "You're not going anywhere. What did you tell her, Tina?"

Tina wrung her hands together. "It's okay, Cor. She promised not to tell anyone about us."

Head smack. This woman couldn't be for real. I tried to laugh it off. "Tell anyone what? I've forgotten already."

Corey backed me up against the wall. He pressed his face so close to mine that I could count the veins bulging in his forehead. "Who do you think you are?" he demanded as his hot, sour breath invaded my nostrils. "It's bad enough that we've had to stay in this crappy town for too long and my whole production schedule is shot. Now we've got a Nancy Drew wannabee adding to our problems, making things difficult as well. You'd better stick to baking cookies, honey."

Sweat, the result of fear, gathered in the small of my back. The man scared me, but I couldn't let him know it. "This is all a misunderstanding—"

We were interrupted by a knock on the door. Relief swept over me like a tidal wave. "Brian!" I screamed.

"Sally?" Brian called. "Are you okay?" He started to pound on the door. "Open at once! This is the police!"

Corey muttered a curse word but released his hold on me. I couldn't open the door fast enough and ran straight into Brian. "He—he tried to hurt me," I sputtered.

"I barely touched her!" Corey yelled. "She was here playing private detective. I don't appreciate your underhanded tactics, Detective."

Brian ignored him and grabbed me by the shoulders. "Are you okay?"

I nodded. "Please, let's go."

But Brian wasn't finished yet. "Wait here," he instructed me.

Before I could even attempt a reply, Brian pushed Corey back into the room and slammed the door behind them. Whatever he said to Corey was in a low tone, impossible for me to hear. Two minutes later, Brian emerged, looking exactly the same except for a faint color rising in his cheeks.

He took me by the elbow and rang for the elevator. "*Now* we're done here."

"What did you say to him?" I asked.

Brian didn't answer. Once we had reached the lobby, he took my elbow protectively as we walked outside to his car. Was he angry with me? Heck, at least this hadn't been my idea for once! "Would you please tell me what's going on?" I asked.

He opened the passenger door for me. Once I was safely inside, Brian walked around and got behind the wheel then turned to face me. "Sally, I owe you an apology. It was a mistake to get you involved. I thought Corey had checked out of the hotel. If something had happened to you—" He broke off. "It was a stupid thing for me to do."

I was so shocked by his words that it took a minute for me to respond. "It's not your fault. I wanted to come. He was just trying to scare me." Maybe. "What did you say to him?"

Brian started the engine. "I threatened to arrest him for attempted assault if he didn't level with me about Smiley's death. He insisted that he didn't have anything to do with it. Then he gave me the name of the man he thinks did."

"Slim?" I guessed.

Brian shook his head. "Corey said that they did a taping for the show in Syracuse last week, and Hal Derby made a surprise visit to the set to see his client. Corey said that Smiley was pretty shaken up after he left."

"Where do we find this guy?" I asked.

"Forget it, Sally." Brian drove out of the lot. "I don't want you involved in this anymore."

"I can't walk away now," I protested. "There's too much at stake for me!"

Brian stared straight ahead. "Forget it. I can't believe I was so stupid. That was a dumb thing for me to do. And I don't want to have to answer to Mike if something happens to you. Thanks for the offer, but I'll manage on my own."

"What did Corey say about Hal?" I persisted. "Does he know where to find him?"

Brian let out an exasperated sigh. "You never quit. All right, if it makes you happy, Corey said he knows the circle Hal travels in. I guess this wasn't the first time he'd heard the bookie's name mentioned. Then I told Corey it was in his best interest to stick around for a while. And I might have mentioned possible assault charges. That seemed to get his attention."

He pulled his car into my driveway. "Now, what exactly did you say to Tina? She was practically foaming at the mouth when I left."

"Hmm. I might have told a little lie and said that we had started out like her and Corey." Heat flooded my cheeks, and Brian avoided my eyes. "Hey, it worked! At least until Corey came to the door."

Brian rewarded me with a smile. "Did she say anything else?"

"She told me that Smiley knew about their relationship. I guess he was always cracking stupid jokes at their expense, and it made Corey furious."

"I figured it was something like that," Brian mused. "Corey must have been afraid Smiley would tell his wife."

"Smiley could have been blackmailing him for money," I said. "God knows he needed it."

Brian scratched his head. "That's a good theory. You're not bad—for a Nancy Drew wannabee, that is."

"Did Corey tell you that he called me that?"

"No," Brian laughed. "I've always connected you with Nancy Drew in my head. Honestly, though? I think you're a much better detective than she is. Now, get out of my car and go enjoy the rest of the day with your family."

"That's high praise coming from a newly minted detective," I teased.

* * *

"Have you heard anything about Smiley's service?" my father asked me at dinner that evening. "Did his wife pick out a funeral home yet? I could use a high-profile service like his right now."

"Jeez, Dad," Gianna said in disgust. "A man just died, and all you can think about is how to profit by it."

Dad poured himself another glass of wine from the decanter. "But that's what I do!" he said. "I'm a businessman at heart."

Grandma Rosa came into the room with a tureen full of braciole and sauce. "Show some respect, Domenic. All you care about is undertaking the man's funeral."

"Nice pun, Grandma," I chuckled.

She wrinkled her brow, so I knew it hadn't been intentional. To my surprise, she said nothing further and returned to the kitchen. Her behavior troubled me lately, and I wondered if she was feeling ill.

"Hey," Dad protested. "Times are hard. I need to make a living, and no one's been dying lately. Something's got to give. Sal, you talked to his wife, right? Did you put in a good word for me?"

I helped myself to some antipasto. "No, Dad. I didn't even think about it."

My father acted as if I had mortally wounded him. "Thanks a lot," he grumbled. "It's a sad state of affairs when a man's own family doesn't care about him or his profession."

Mike glared at my father. "Sorry, Dom, but some things

take precedence, like Sal almost getting attacked today. I'd love to go down to the Hilton and straighten that guy out for myself."

Gianna refilled her wineglass. "I can't believe that you want Sal to talk to Smiley's widow, Dad. I mean, the man was beaten to death in her bakery. Show a little compassion."

My father swiped a piece of Italian bread through the remaining tomato sauce on his plate and stuffed it into his mouth. "Compassion doesn't pay the bills, my beautiful daughter. Birds gonna fly, and people gotta die."

My mother collapsed into a fit of giggles. "Domenic, you are so clever." She beamed at all of us. "He's a poet, and he didn't even know it."

Johnny groaned. "You guys are killing me."

"Do you know anything about the DNA findings at the crime scene?" Gianna asked me. "The police should have found something on the killer, unless he or she wore gloves."

I helped myself to some linguini. "Brian said that they did find evidence but couldn't make a match. It sounds like whoever killed Smiley didn't have a prior record. My feeling is this might have been a crime of passion. Maybe the person didn't originally set out to kill Smiley." If so, what could have happened that led to his being beaten to death with a rolling pin?

Grandma Rosa sat down next to me with a cup of demitasse. I reached over and touched her hand. She jumped slightly. "Are you feeling okay?"

"I am fine, dear girl," she said quietly.

Something was going on. "You don't seem like yourself lately."

"She's just upset about her trip," Dad volunteered.

"You might still be able to go," I said hopefully.

She gave me a wistful smile. "There are some things that we do not have control over in this life. Everything happens for a reason, *cara mia."*

My heart ached for her. It was obvious my grandmother had been looking forward to the trip as much as Mrs. Gavelli had. "I'd love to see you be able to go back to Italy and experience everything all over again."

Grandma Rosa shook her head. "Things do not work that way. We can never recapture things that happened fifty years ago in the same manner again." She stared out the window, and I was struck by the sadness in her eyes. "It was not meant to be."

Chatter at the dinner table continued around us while my grandmother's words kept echoing in my head. The anticipated trip to Italy had awakened some past memories for Grandma Rosa, and it pained me to see her in such a melancholy state. When she'd stated that it wasn't meant to be, I couldn't help wondering if she was talking about the trip or something else instead. I'd give anything to see her experience the happiness that she so richly deserved.

CHAPTER FOURTEEN

Josie's face contorted with worry. "Oh my God, Sal, that must have been so scary. What if Corey had hurt you?"

"It was scary," I admitted. "But it's over with now."

Josie was silent as she rolled out dough with our new rolling pin. "I hope so."

"Let's focus on the positive." I stretched my arms out wide. "We're back in our bakery, and we actually had customers this morning."

"Yeah, three," Josie said sourly. "And one of them was Nicoletta, so she doesn't count."

Mondays were usually a busy day as we were closed on Sundays, but this one had a morbid and depressing feel to it. Smiley's murder still haunted me and probably would for a long time. Although we'd cleaned the entire area from top to bottom, it was difficult to walk around without picturing his lifeless body lying on the floor.

I'd half expected to see Jerry outside the shop with a camera crew this morning when we'd opened. If he had shown up, I might have been tempted to shove the microphone down his throat. With Josie, there was no maybe involved. She definitely would make it happen.

We had spent the afternoon working on a new recipe that Josie recently created. Her fudgy cosmic brownie cookies were to die for, and I knew that they would be popular with graduation parties right around the corner. The second time Josie made the batter, I had the recipe down. They were about double the size of our usual cookies, and Josie suggested we price them at four dollars apiece.

"We have to do it, Sal," she said. "We should also start increasing the size of our cookies to go along with the price. We've got a lot of competition out there."

It was a good idea in theory, only now we had no customers to purchase them. A few orders for cookie trays were trickling in for the busy summer season, but nowhere near as many as we usually received.

Josie worked in silence for a few minutes before she slammed her hand down on a stainless steel tray. "This is ridiculous. We've been in business for almost five years, and our customers should have more faith in us. Why are people so fickle?"

"It won't stay like this," I assured her, but doubt continued to nag at my brain. I had a new house to pay for, and I wanted to put Cookie in a toddler school program this fall that was going to cost us a small fortune. It would be difficult to place her with strangers at first, but I had a business to run and couldn't keep depending on Johnny and my grandmother to take care of her while I worked, especially since Alex would be going to school as well. It was a four day a week program, and I planned to take Fridays off to spend with her while Dodie helped Josie.

Josie didn't answer. Her situation was more precarious than mine. She had four kids to my one and many more expenses to deal with.

"We'll just have to take it one day at a time." I tried to make light of the situation. "In the meantime, there's more of these fudgy cookies for me to eat."

We laughed as the bells on the front door jingled, announcing that we had a customer. Josie dusted her hands off on her apron. "I'll see who it is."

"Hopefully someone who wants to buy half of our display case." We'd have to cut back on our supply of cookies. There was no point in making all the different varieties when no one was around to buy them. With a sigh, I removed a tray of fortune cookies from the oven.

"Sal." Josie's voice sounded uneasy. "Someone is here to see you."

I washed my hands in the sink and went into the storefront. A tall, imposing man with ash-blond hair wearing an expensive navy suit was gazing into the display case with interest. He straightened up when I came into the room.

"Can I help you?"

He stretched his hand out. "Hal Derby. I heard that you were asking around about me."

My mouth went dry. Hal was not at all what I figured a loan shark would look like. I had expected a man similar to one found in a gangster-type movie. He was an attractive man in his mid-forties with nearly perfect features, but there was something about his demeanor that made me nervous.

Hal nodded politely at Josie and me with a smile that didn't quite reach his eyes. They were a pale gray, almost colorless, and as cold as ice cubes. A shiver ran down my spine.

I had no choice but to clasp the cool hand that he had extended. "It's very nice to meet you, but I wasn't—"

"The pleasure is all mine," he interrupted briskly. "What can I do for you?"

Crap. This was not the way it should have played out. Hal was supposed to contact Brian, or vice versa. Corey must have mentioned my name to him.

Josie watched me anxiously. I swallowed hard and tried to stay calm. "Yes, I heard that you knew Smiley Jones. We're trying to find out what happened to him."

He wrinkled his brow. "I heard that he died here—in your bakery. Someone bashed his head in with a rolling pin."

Hal didn't believe in mincing words. "I was told that you were a friend of Smiley's."

He gave me a blank stare, so I tried again. "Okay, what I meant to say is, you saw him recently. I was wondering if you knew anything about his personal life. Did he—"

"Mrs. Donovan, I am a businessman, first and foremost," Hal cut in. "I don't have *friends,* nor do I want any. Smiley was a client. When he died, he owed me a lot of dough." The corners of his mouth quivered. "No pun intended."

"None taken," Josie chimed in nervously.

He pointed at the raspberry cheesecake cookies in the case. "Those look good."

"Please give Mr. Derby a cookie, Jos."

Josie immediately sprang into action and looked grateful to be busy. Hal watched as she grabbed a piece of waxed paper to remove the cookie from the case and handed it to him.

Hal took a bite and closed his eyes as he chewed. "Delicious. You ladies certainly know what you're doing."

Josie's face relaxed at the praise, and I decided to try another tactic. "I was told that you saw Smiley shortly before he died. Did he seem anxious or upset to you?"

"Sorry, Mrs. Donovan. I don't discuss my clients, dead or alive. All I care about is the money owed to me. Someone else will have to compensate for Smiley's debt. Do you understand? The bills just don't go away when a client dies. That's not how I roll." Hal smiled again, obviously delighted with his sense of humor.

"We heard that Smiley had a huge life insurance policy," Josie volunteered.

I knew Josie only said this to see if Hal was aware of the policy, and I silently applauded her efforts.

"Who told you that?" Hal's voice was as cold and as rough as the northern wind in January.

"Oh, we heard everyone talking about it at the casino the other night. No one seems to know who the beneficiary is, though," I lied.

Hal thought about this as he took another bite of his cookie. He nodded towards Josie. "Give me a dozen of these to go, please."

Josie assembled a pink bakery box and quickly filled it with the cookies. She cocked an eyebrow at me as if to say, *This is getting us nowhere.*

To my surprise, Hal spoke up. "His wife."

"Excuse me?" I asked.

Hal turned his opaque gaze on me. "His wife is the beneficiary. Angela."

"How do you know?" I asked.

"Because I make it my business to know these things." Hal finished his cookie and wiped a crumb off his white silk tie. "When people owe me money, I like to know that there's a backup plan, so to speak. She'll be hearing from me soon."

"Did you ever loan money to anyone else from the *Senior Moments* show?" I asked.

Hal's face froze like a statue. "I might have. But as I already told you, that's strictly my business."

"Please, Mr. Derby," I said. "We're only trying to find out who might have killed Smiley. Look around you. My bakery is suffering because of what happened to him. You're a businessman, so you understand what I'm going through. People don't want to come back here until they're sure it's safe. We won't tell a soul, honest."

Josie tied string around the box and handed it to him.

"The cookies are on the house, by the way."

Hal glanced from Josie to me, and his features softened. He pushed the twine back from the box and reached inside for a cookie. This time, he popped the entire one into his mouth and chewed, slowly and thoughtfully. It was unnerving and seemed to go on forever.

"Did you loan money to a man named Slim?" I persisted. "Dark hair, angular face, rail-thin build? He was at Let it Ride the other night."

Hal didn't even blink. He picked up his cookies and walked towards the front door. Josie glanced at me helplessly, and I shrugged in return. As Grandma Rosa always said, food was the way to a man's stomach. I think she meant heart, but that worked too.

Hal stopped at the door but didn't turn around. Josie and I both waited, not daring to breathe. After what felt like an eternity, he finally spoke. "Merriweather. First name, Miles." The silver bells jingled merrily, and he was gone.

* * *

"That guy gives me the creeps." Josie shivered as she stared out the front window, watching the clouds roll in. "Look at how dark the sky is getting, and it's only four o'clock. Either we're going to get one whopper of a storm tonight, or Hal Derby's weird vibrations are responsible."

"He's not a witch," I laughed. "Only a loan shark. But I think your cookies have made him a kinder, gentler soul."

She winked. "I don't know about that. Hal's been gone for over an hour, and I'm still shaking. Don't tell me he didn't make you nervous."

There was no point in denying it. "Sure, he was a little scary, but he gave us the information that we needed. And we knew that Slim had to be some kind of a nickname."

"Miles Merriweather? Jonas Jones? Heck, those parents must not have liked their kids very much," Josie declared.

"I can see why he might have picked Slim for a nickname. It's a variation of Miles. Which is also a variation of Smiley, without the y."

"It is a weird coincidence," Josie admitted, "and makes me think that they both knew each other on a more personal level.

Of course, I'm also curious what they had to hide, besides their original names. Did you text Brian?"

"Yes, but I don't expect to hear from him for a while. Brian sent me a text earlier that he had to leave town for the day. I guess his father is in the hospital. Nothing life threatening, but today was the only chance he had to see him." Like a maze, new ideas were running through my mind. "Maybe we could find Slim—I mean Miles—ourselves."

Josie's jaw dropped. "But Sal, what if he's the one who killed Smiley? You don't know anything about him. And I can't ride shotgun tonight. Danny's got a baseball game, and I promised to be there."

"No worries. Maybe we could try tomorrow."

Her expression turned sheepish. "I hate to ask, but would you mind closing up by yourself? It's an away game and will take me at least thirty minutes to get there."

"Not at all," I said. "You've been at it since six o'clock this morning. Go ahead and take off, and I'll finish up."

"Are you sure?" she asked. "I know you're not feeling well. By the way, when is your doctor's appointment?"

"The day after tomorrow." I was trying not to think about it and kept telling myself that anemia was the reason I felt so tired all the time. "And I feel fine. Go catch the game, and wish Danny good luck for me."

Josie shot me a grateful smile. "All right, if you insist. It'll be nice to see an entire game from the beginning for once." She swung her purse over her shoulder and opened the back door that led to the alley. "Night, Sal."

"Have a good one." I stepped across the room and locked the door behind her. There wasn't much left to do in the bakery. I removed the little money from the register and placed it in a night bag to drop at the bank before I went home. There were a few utensils left in the sink to wash. Afterwards, I swept the floors and double-checked that the ovens were off. The wall clock read four forty-five. There was still fifteen minutes to go before closing time. With a sigh, I went to the front window. The sky had turned black, and raindrops were spattering against the glass. *Oh, the heck with it. No one else is coming in today.* I turned out the lights, set the alarm, and closed the kitchen door behind me.

Raindrops pelted me as I made my way to the car. A sudden gust of wind blew an avalanche of dust into my eyes while I unlocked the door. As I threw my items in the back seat and attempted to wipe my eyes, someone grabbed me from behind. Panicked, I tried to scream, but a hand clamped down firmly on my mouth.

"Do what I say, and you won't get hurt." The voice was deep and undistinguishable. The person said something else, but it was difficult to hear over the rain and howling wind. My attacker quickly grew impatient and gripped my arms tighter. "I said, nod once if you understand."

Fear swept over me, and I managed a quick nod.

"Now, you're going to get in my trunk, and we'll go someplace to have a little talk," the voice said. "Because you're getting to be a problem."

I tried to struggle, but my assailant responded by wrapping a thick arm around my neck. Terrified, I dug my heels into the ground and began to claw at the skin underneath the sleeve, but the person was much stronger than me. The arm tightened around my neck, threatening to cut off my air supply.

"Knock it off, or you're gonna be sorry!"

Out of the corner of my eye, I glimpsed a sedan through the torrent of rain. It was either dark blue or black. My attacker stopped next to the trunk, their arm still securely wrapped around my neck. "If you want to live, you'll get in. Don't try anything, or I'll kill you right here."

I dug my heels in again, refusing to budge.

"Get in," the person hissed and tried to lift me off the ground.

At that moment, something inside of me snapped. Maybe I would wind up dead, but I wasn't going down without a fight. The worst thing I could ever do was get inside the vehicle, because there was an excellent chance I would never make it out again.

My assailant grunted and delivered a sharp blow to the side of my face. My ears began to ring as a numbing pain set in. Nearly blinded from the pain, I almost lost consciousness. As my attacker placed their hand over my mouth again, I didn't hesitate. I bit down on their thumb as hard as I could. They let out a shrieking howl and immediately loosened their grip enough so I could break free. There was no time to waste. I ran as fast as I could, directly into the path of the storm. My clothes were soaked through, but my only conscious thought was how to make it out of this experience alive.

"Help!" I screamed against the wind, in a vain attempt that someone might hear. "Please help me!"

CHAPTER FIFTEEN

As I ran through the alley, I expected to hear the popping sound of a gun, but it never came. I didn't dare turn around to see if my attacker was following. The rain had become a torrential downpour, and I could barely see two feet in front of me. I stopped briefly at the side of the road, searching for car lights, and then plunged across and up the sloping hill to my house.

I was literally running for my life.

My lungs were near bursting as I ran through the wet grass. I lost a sneaker in a muddy puddle of water but continued on. Nothing would stop me now.

Grandma Rosa was at my house, watching Cookie today. I'd left my keys and purse in the car, so I began to bang on the front door. "Grandma! Let me in!"

The door was opened quickly, and I rushed inside. Grandma Rosa stood there in amazement, watching as I quickly locked the door behind me. "What is wrong?" she asked worriedly.

"Police," I managed to say in between gulps of air. "Call them."

"My dear girl, are you all right? What has happened?"

"Someone—tried to—to grab—me." I was panting and sweating profusely, despite the fact that I'd was soaked from head to toe. "Please call them, Grandma."

Grandma Rosa hurried to grab her cell and dialed 9-1-1. "Sit down, *cara mia*, and rest." My grandmother placed the afghan that she'd crocheted for me around my shoulders and went into the kitchen with her phone. After about five minutes, she returned with a steaming mug of tea that she handed to me. "Drink this."

I took a long sip from the mug as she sat down at my side, her soulful brown eyes full of concern. "The police are on their way. Now tell me. This has something to do with Mr. Jones's death, doesn't it? Who tried to hurt you?"

Quickly, I explained what had transpired. "Yes. I'm sure it has to do with Smiley's death. And I couldn't see their face, so I have no idea who it was." My mind was racing with all kinds of ideas. Corey was the most logical choice, but what about Angela or Slim? I still didn't know what his motive might be, though.

Grandma Rosa shook her head soberly. "My dear girl, do you realize how lucky you were tonight? The angels were watching over you."

Truer words were never spoken. "Where's Cookie?" I asked suddenly.

"She just went to sleep," Grandma Rosa explained. "The dear baby refused to nap earlier and was very cranky. I hope that she will sleep through the night for you, but maybe not. Now, you need some dry clothes. And some more hot tea." She helped me rise from the couch.

"Thanks, Grandma." I leaned heavily against her with a hope that some of her enduring strength might seep into my body.

Grandma Rosa kissed my cheek. "Get changed, my dear, and then come out to the kitchen. I am certain the police will be here soon."

I went into the master bathroom and quickly stripped out of my clothes then dried myself all over with a soft, thick towel. As much as I longed for a shower, there wasn't time. I went into my adjoining bedroom and pulled on a hooded sweatshirt, jeans, and my favorite fuzzy socks. When I walked into the kitchen five minutes later, Officer Walden was sitting there, talking to Grandma Rosa and drinking a mug of tea. She set another one in front of me.

Officer Walden rose and nodded to me. "Mrs. Donovan, your grandmother said that someone tried to abduct you. What can you tell me?"

"Not much," I admitted and relayed what had happened. "Then he, or maybe she, said, 'I think you know what this is about.' That I was getting to be a problem and we needed to have a talk." The words still made me shiver.

"Was it a man or woman?" Officer Walden wanted to know.

I shrugged. "Hard to say. The rain was coming down heavy, and I couldn't distinguish their tone and words. They were much stronger than me, though."

"Almost everyone is," Grandma Rosa put in.

Jeez, thanks a lot. "Well, you would have been proud of me, Grandma. I left them with a nice mark on their thumb that won't be going away for a while."

"Good for you," Officer Walden said approvingly. "What do you think your attacker meant when they said you were getting to be a problem? Could it have had something to do with Smiley Jones's murder in your bakery?"

Officer Walden wasn't Brian, so there was no way he'd automatically deduce that the two incidents were related. "Yes, I'm positive of it."

The front door slammed, and Mike's anxious voice filled the house. "Sal! Where are you?"

"We are in the kitchen," Grandma Rosa called back and nodded at me. "I phoned Mike while you were getting changed."

Mike rushed into the kitchen and lifted me up from the chair in a single swoop, wrapping his strong arms around me. "Are you all right, princess? Did he hurt you?"

"No, I'm fine." The anxious look in his eyes almost reduced me to tears. I sucked in a deep breath and tried to pull myself together.

Officer Walden rose from his chair and extended a hand. "Mr. Donovan, I'm Officer Walden."

"Thank you for coming out." Mike sat down heavily next to me and reached for my hand. "I don't believe this. You could have been killed!"

I clasped his hand in mine. "Everything's okay now."

"But for how long?" Mike wanted to know as Grandma Rosa brought him some tea. "That lunatic is going to come after you again."

There was another knock, and the door opened. My mother called out, "Sal, honey? Are you okay?"

I turned to my grandmother. "Jeez, you work fast."

She nodded gravely. "You need your family around you at a time like this, *cara mia*. Even the nutsy cookie ones."

Officer Walden looked up from the note he was scribbling. He blinked, shook his head, and kept on writing.

My parents came into the kitchen, followed by Gianna. She threw her arms around me. "Sal!" she cried. "I was at Mom and Dad's when Grandma called and said someone had tried to attack you. What happened?"

A wail burst from the baby monitor on the table.

My mother held up a finger. "Stay here, sweetie. I'll go and take care of that precious angel."

"You were lucky, baby girl." My father's voice became hoarse with emotion. "I don't know what we would have done if—" He broke off suddenly and ruffled my hair.

A lump came to my throat, and I patted his hand. Sure, my parents might be a bit loony at times, but I had never doubted their love for me and Gianna. They were always there when we needed them. And Grandma Rosa was in a class all by herself.

"Do you think it could have been Corey from Smiley's show?" Gianna asked.

My father nodded. "Yep. I just saw a Facebook post about him and his girlfriend. Apparently, someone leaked their affair to the press. It said that she works on the set of *Senior Moments*."

The details hadn't taken long to surface. "He's definitely a possibility. Smiley knew about Corey's affair and might have been threatening to tell his wife."

Gianna wrinkled her nose. "He's married? What a creep."

"That's right," Dad said cheerfully as he opened my fridge and hunted around inside it. "Someone snuck a photo of him leaving the hotel with her. The article said her name's Tina something. I'll bet that Jerry Maroon was behind it."

I uttered a curse word under my breath. "Great. Corey's going to think I had something to do with the photo."

"Why would he think that?" Gianna asked.

"Because he showed up at the hotel while I was talking to Tina," I explained. "When he found out that I was asking questions and Tina had told me about their affair, he grabbed me and threatened to—"

Mike clenched his fists. "Every time you mention that guy, I want to track him down and rearrange his face."

Officer Walden cleared his throat uncomfortably and rose from the table. "Mrs. Donovan, I'm glad that you're all right. I'll go over to the bakery and check out your car for any clues. But since you can't identify your attacker, there isn't much else we can do at the moment."

"Yes, I understand. Thank you for coming by."

My father, who had found some leftover pizza in the

fridge, took a bite from a slice and gestured at the officer. "I'll show you out, son. And then I'll run over in a couple of minutes and bring Sal's car back here."

"Thanks, Dad."

After they had left the room, Mike started to pace around the table. "I knew this was going to happen, Sal. Your life is constantly in danger."

"It is not her fault, my dear boy," Grandma Rosa said simply. "Sally and murder go together like an ocean and the Titanic."

Yikes. Not an image I wanted to envision.

"That's not really flattering, Grandma," Gianna said.

"It doesn't matter." Mike put his cup in the sink. "Whoever killed Smiley knows that you've been going around asking questions, and now your life is in danger."

"Who have you talked to so far?" Gianna wanted to know. "That could give us an idea of the person responsible for his death and who might be trying to hurt you."

I gulped down the rest of my tea. "Josie and I talked to Smiley's wife Angela. They were in the process of getting divorced, and she stands to inherit a million-dollar life insurance policy. Then Brian and I went to the Hilton—" I hesitated, not wanting to tell Mike the part about us pretending we were married. "That's where I talked to Tina, the makeup girl. She told me that Smiley was always giving Corey a hard time about the affair. It's possible he might have been blackmailing Corey with the information."

"Anyone else?" Gianna asked.

"Yes, a man named Hal Derby. He's a bookie who Smiley owed a lot of money to." I went on to enlighten them about the visit Hal had paid to my bakery today.

Gianna raised an eyebrow. "Wow. You have been busy."

"No one's been able to find Slim," I continued. "And we found out that his real name is Miles Merriweather."

Gianna removed a manila folder from her purse. "If you want, I can have a background check run on him as well. I had one done for Smiley, even though the police probably have all his information already. I know his death has been horrible for the bakery and you, so I wanted to help."

"I appreciate that," I said. "What does it say?"

She traced her finger down the page. "Let's see. He grew

up in the Buffalo area and owns a house in Rochester and one in Florida."

"Guess again," I said. "He lost the home in Florida due to gambling debts. Where did he go to college?"

Gianna squinted down at the report. "There's no college mentioned. It says that he graduated from McKinstry High School. That's less than half an hour from here."

My father had returned to the kitchen and peered over Gianna's shoulder. "Poor guy," he lamented. "Never even made it to his fiftieth birthday. That's when all the fun starts."

Gianna narrowed her eyes. "It says that he had a clean record until about three years ago. That's when he was high and hit the other car."

"And killed one of the passengers inside," I finished. "Brian already filled me in on all the lovely details, remember?"

"But it really makes me sick," Gianna admitted. "If he'd been my client, I'd have left him in the courtroom to defend himself. The ones who are rich and powerful always end up buying themselves out of trouble."

"It might be worth it to go check the high school out," I said.

Mike stared at me in disbelief. "Sal, he graduated over twenty-five years ago. What would you expect to find out there?"

"No idea, but I've got to try." I removed the manila envelope from my purse and withdrew the playing cards. "Check it out. These are the cards that Smiley mailed to me. The ace of spades means death. Plain and simple."

Gianna picked up the queen of spades card and studied it. "What about this one?"

"I looked it up online. There are a couple of variations, but for the most part, it means a strong and intelligent woman." Angela immediately came to mind.

"But why did he have to send the cards to you?" Mike asked. "Couldn't he have called someone for help if he knew his life was in danger?"

"Smiley said that he'd send me an autographed picture. Maybe he slipped the cards in at the last moment because he worried something was going to happen to him." I thought about the fortune cookie he'd received with no message in it that evening. The signs were all there, but I hadn't seen them.

A gleam of excitement flickered through my father's

eyes. "Count me in for whatever you have planned. I'm all set to take on the person who tried to attack my baby girl."

Gianna and I exchanged a glance. There was no way that I'd let my father get involved with this mess. He meant well, but he always ended up making things worse, if this could even get any worse.

I picked up my cell. "Thanks, Dad, but I need to call Josie and see if she'll run a little errand with me tomorrow morning."

"Sal," Mike objected. "Don't tempt fate again. Please."

I leaned over and kissed him. "I promise this is nothing for you to worry about. I only want to make a trip to Smiley's high school in Buffalo."

He gave me a strange look. "Why? It sounds like a waste of time to me."

I didn't have time to answer him since Josie picked up at that moment. "What's going on, partner?"

With a deep breath, I quickly explained what had happened and placed special emphasis on the fact that I was all right. Josie reacted much as I'd expected. "Oh my God, Sal! They could have killed you! This is all my fault for leaving early—"

"Stop right there," I interrupted. "You had nothing to do with it. Okay, moving on. How do you feel about leaving Dodie in charge of the bakery tomorrow morning and running an errand with me?"

She hesitated for a moment on the other end. "It depends. Does this have anything to do with Smiley's murder?"

"Yes."

"I figured it did." Josie paused. "Well, there's always a chance that she might burn the bakery down while we're gone, but I would never desert you in your hour of need."

"I knew that I could count on you."

"Girlfriend, I'll never let you down," Josie said. "Not while there's a breath left in my body."

CHAPTER SIXTEEN

The McKinstry High School building was in the shape of the letter *C*. One side was devoted to junior high students, and the other two for upper classmen. The statistics I brought up on my phone indicated that there were about 2,000 students in grades nine through twelve. It was a far cry from Colwestern High School, which Josie, Mike, and I had all attended and its impressive graduating class of sixty.

Josie found a parking spot in the public lot, and we walked along the sidewalk to the entrance, getting a few curious glances from students who were outside, either chatting or involved in passionate embraces. I nudged her. "Doesn't that bring back memories?"

A smile tugged at the corners of her mouth. "Yep, so like me. Skipping class at ten in the morning to meet Rob outside."

"You were such a bad influence on me," I teased.

She laughed. "Oh, please. You were too busy running down the halls after Mike."

"True," I admitted. "But hey, it paid off."

The main entrance was locked, so we rang the doorbell. A woman was sitting near the door at a table typing on a laptop. She rose and pressed a button on the wall, speaking to us through an intercom device. "Can I help you?"

"Hello," I called back. "We'd like to see about getting a copy of a yearbook. Do you keep them here?"

She raised her eyebrows at me. "We do, but they're not for sale. Were you a student here?"

"No," I admitted, "but—"

"Well, then, I'm terribly sorry but you'll have to—" The woman's gaze shifted to Josie and her eyes widened in pleasure. "Oh! You're the one who made my daughter's wedding cake last year."

Josie's face lit up like a firework. "That's right. Ava Seymour, right?"

The woman nodded and quickly opened the door. "You have a good memory. She got so many compliments on the cake. Ava hated to cut into it because it was so lovely. Come on in—both of you."

Once we were inside the building, she locked the door behind us and gestured at a clipboard on the table. "Please sign in here."

After we had done so, the woman pointed at a narrow hallway filled with lockers on both sides. "If you go through the Norris Wing, you'll see a double set of doors. After that you'll come to the library. Miss Dunham will help you."

We thanked her and started down the hallway. It was empty, except for one student rummaging through his locker. The murmur on the other side of classroom doors struck a familiar chord and filled me with nostalgia. "Jeez, it feels just like yesterday."

Josie made a face. "For you, maybe. It feels like another lifetime for me. And I'm glad because I for one hated school."

On that cheerful note, we entered the library and spotted a silver-haired woman behind the front counter. She was directing a student to another area of the room. When he walked away, she turned to us with a smile. "May I help you?"

"Are you Miss Dunham?" I asked.

"That's right. What can I do for you?"

I cleared my throat. "We were wondering if we might be able to view some of your yearbooks."

The woman's angular face studied us closely. "Were you former students here?"

For some reason, I decided to level with her. "No. We're looking into the death of Smiley Jones. We understand that he went to school here."

"Oh." Miss Dunham's expression turned sober. "So, you're police officers?"

Josie rolled her eyes toward the ceiling while I smiled pleasantly at the woman. "No, but we were personal friends of his. Did you know him by chance?"

The librarian shook her head. "Afraid not. By the time that I started working here, he'd been graduated for about ten years or so. He's one of only a couple of celebrities who attended our school, so he's kind of a big deal to us. And it was so nice of him to come back and speak to the school last month."

"He did?" I hadn't counted on this stroke of luck. "Do you remember exactly what day he was here?"

She turned and examined a calendar on the wall. "Let's see. I remember that it was the day after the assembly we had on Earth Day, so—wait. Yes, it was April 23rd. We have at least two assemblies a week for the students. He talked to them about his television career and was most entertaining. The students loved him."

Only three weeks ago. "Do you happen to remember if—"

Miss Dunham held up a finger. "Wait one second." We stood there and watched as she approached a nearby desk and lifted a picture frame from the surface. With a radiant smile, she leaned over the counter and handed it to me. The photo was of her with a grinning Smiley. He had an arm casually slung around her shoulders.

"He was a lovely man, and it was so sweet of him to pose for a photo with me." Miss Dunham clucked her tongue against the roof of her mouth. "We were all saddened to learn about his death. Was it really murder?"

I nodded. "Yes, I'm afraid so."

She shook her head and removed the frame from my hands. "And they have no idea who could have done such a thing?"

"Not that we're aware of," I said. "If there's any significant details that you remember from the day he was here—even if it seems small—that could help us to determine who killed him."

"Honestly, I can't think of anything," Miss Dunham admitted. "Mr. Jones talked to the kids for about forty-five minutes, answered some questions, and posed for photos. Then he said he had to leave and catch a plane to Maryland. I believe he was shooting another episode of *Senior Moments* the next day."

"And he seemed normal?" Josie asked.

Miss Dunham shot her a strange look. "Why, yes, he acted perfectly fine. Did you still want to see the yearbooks? I'm guessing you're looking for the editions that would have Mr. Jones in them. I'm not sure of the exact years, but—"

"My best guess would be either 1999 or 2000," I said.

"We'd love to see if there's any files on him from his school career as well."

"Well, the yearbooks are available to the public and you can look at those," Miss Dunham said. "But student files are confidential." She lifted a flap in the counter and walked past us, her heelless sandals making a squishing noise against the carpet. "They're all over here." She pointed at a bookcase that had a table and chairs in front of it.

"Do you even have student files for back then?" I asked.

"We have paper files," she answered. "They go back to the 1970s. The school didn't switch to electronic until about fifteen years ago. Paper files are all kept in a storage facility offsite."

We thanked her, and she walked away, leaving us to our own devices. I handed the 2000 yearbook to Josie then sat down and went to work on the1999 edition. I immediately found the Seniors section and started to flip through the pages. The photos for the upperclassmen were larger than the rest of the grades. Each graduate took up a quarter of the page.

"Look at this." Josie leaned over my shoulder, pointing at one girl who was positioned against a tree, with the high school looming in the background. "At least they didn't have to wear those dorky drapes like we did. And they got to do cool poses outside by the picnic tables. Our school should have had something more modern."

"They were always behind the times." I turned my attention back to the yearbook and thumbed through several pages until I came to the J's. In the upper right-hand corner was the photo I'd been looking for. "Look, it's him!"

A young Smiley stared back at me from between the cream-colored pages. He was dressed in a tan blazer and white dress shirt, with dark hair parted straight down the middle. His trademark grin was marred by a mouthful of metal.

"Good thing his parents could afford braces," Josie mused. "The name Smiley doesn't exactly work well with crooked teeth."

Underneath Smiley's photo was a summary of his high school activities. From the looks of things, he'd been very active then. *Jonas William Jones. Debate club president, senior class president, honor student, golf club, President of card playing club.*

Josie snickered. "The last one was a given."

Underneath Smiley's activities, his class motto was listed. *Life is all about luck.*

"We should have known," Josie sighed.

I went to the activity section of the yearbook, hoping to spot some more pictures of Smiley. I found him posing with the rest of the golf club team, dressed in white shorts and a sweater vest, grinning as if his life depended on it.

"He looks like your typical prep," Josie noted. "Sal, what exactly are you trying to find? These photos are over twenty years old. They're not going to lead us to his killer."

"Yeah, you're right. Maybe I was hoping that a clue would magically appear. But I guess it's a dead end."

"We know that he was deep in debt and had made some enemies along the way," Josie observed. "That would ruin anyone's day."

I flipped the pages back to Smiley's senior picture for one last look before putting the yearbook back on the shelf. On the way, I spotted someone familiar in a photo and stopped for a closer look. I sucked in a deep breath.

"Sal, what is it?" Josie asked.

I pointed a trembling finger at the photo. A young man with dark hair was dressed in a black suit and red tie, looking ill at ease. He was standing next to a small stream, the back of the high school visible behind him. His black hair was long and unruly, and he had dark, penetrating eyes that seemed to stare right through me.

It was Miles Merriweather, alias Slim Daniels.

"Holy cow," I whispered. "Smiley and Slim go back a lot further than I thought."

"They had to have known each other then, right?" Josie asked excitedly. "I mean, it's a large school, but—"

I was only half listening as I read through Slim's extracurricular activities. *Miles A. Merriweather. Vice President, card playing club.*

Life is all about luck. His motto was the same as Smiley's.

A chill ran down my spine. "I think we have your answer."

CHAPTER SEVENTEEN

"Okay, let's not jump to conclusions here," Josie said. "Smiley and Slim went to school together and obviously have known each other for a long time. But does that mean he was the one who killed Smiley? Not necessarily. What do you remember about your attacker?"

With dread, I thought back to those fear-filled moments from last night. "It could have been Slim. But I'm not positive it was a man."

"Come on, Sal," Josie said. "There are some obvious differences."

I made a face at her. "Ha ha. Yes, I know what you're saying, but the wind and rain made it difficult to determine the voice. All I can tell you is that the person was stronger and taller than me."

"Taller than you? That's only about ninety-five percent of the population," Josie said cheerfully. "No offense, but you're not helping to narrow the suspects down."

I closed my eyes and tried to think back. "The voice was deep. And whoever they are, they've got a nice bruise on their right thumb from me."

"Angela has a deep voice," Josie observed. "And she also had the most to gain from her husband's death. I thought Smiley's brother might be involved, but Brian keeps insisting he's not."

"It could have been Angela," I admitted. "But Slim has known Smiley for a long time so there might be a connection there as well. Maybe Slim didn't have anything to do with the murder, but he's got to know something. We need to have a talk with him."

Josie placed the yearbooks back on the shelf, and we returned to the front desk.

Miss Dunham was stacking books on the counter as we

approached. She looked up and smiled. "Did you find what you were looking for?" she asked.

"Yes, we found Smiley's photo. Thank you for your help." I paused. "Was there anything else you remembered from the day he visited?"

Miss Dunham shook her head. "I've told you everything I can think of."

"Did Smiley have anyone with him that day?" I persisted. "Maybe his wife or an agent?"

She cocked her head to the side for a second and studied me. "He didn't bring his wife, but another man came with him. I assumed it was his agent, but maybe not. Shoot. What was his name?"

My heart almost leaped out of my chest. "Can you describe him?"

Miss Dunham scrunched her eyebrows together. "Let's see. He was tall and rail thin, with a narrow face. Very polite, but he didn't say much."

"Could his name have been Slim?" I suggested.

She snapped her fingers. "Yes, I do believe that's what it was. Now I remember. Smiley said they were longtime friends. He sat in the back of the auditorium by himself while Smiley gave his speech. When Smiley finished, I thanked him and asked if he would take a photo with me, but I'd left my phone in the library. Thankfully, Smiley had that fellow with him because his friend offered to take the picture and forward it to my phone."

This sounded too good to be true. "Can we see the original text he sent you with the picture? Please, it's important."

Miss Dunham picked up her phone from the desk and scrolled through the contents for a couple of minutes while we waited.

Josie shifted from one foot to another. "Jeez, how many text messages does she get?" she whispered.

"Aha! Here we are." Miss Dunham waved the phone triumphantly in the air.

I leaned over her shoulder for a better look. Smiley was staring back at me with his trademark grin in place. "Could I have a closer look?"

Miss Dunham handed her phone to me. I clicked on the picture, and a phone number came into view. "Jos, can you make a note of this phone number?" I recited the digits to her.

Josie entered the number into her phone, and I returned Miss Dunham's. "Thank you very much for all your help. How did both men seem to get along when they were here?"

Miss Dunham stared at me blankly. "Pardon?"

"I was wondering how Smiley and Slim acted with each other," I explained. "Did they have an argument or anything like that?"

"Why, they got along fine. I didn't notice anything wrong between them." She stared at me with stricken eyes. "You don't think that he's involved in Smiley's murder, do you?"

"We just want to consider every possible angle," Josie explained. "We're aware it's a very serious allegation."

I cocked one eyebrow at her in disbelief. Josie sounded like she was trying to imitate Brian's style. With a great deal of effort, I hid my smile. "We appreciate all that you've done."

Miss Dunham pursed her lips together as if she'd eaten a lemon. "I do hope that the police can find the person responsible for this awful crime. If I can help in any other way, please let me know."

"The killer's name," Josie mumbled as we walked towards my car. "*That's* what we need help with."

I slid behind the wheel and gripped it between my hands as Josie drew her seat belt across her lap. "Sal, what are you doing?"

"I'm trying to figure out where we go from here. Everyone involved has a good motive for wanting Smiley dead."

Josie rubbed her hands together, as if ready to make cookie batter. "All right, let's take stock. Who are our suspects? First, we have Angela Jones. She stood to profit the most with Smiley's life insurance policy. Then there's Corey, who didn't want his wife to know that he was fooling around with Tina. Smiley may have gone too far with his jokes, and Corey worried he'd tell all. Or, Smiley might have blackmailed him. A TV personality extorting money from the director of his show—could it happen?"

"Sure, it could. You can always find another director, but there was only one Smiley."

"Moving on, then." Josie spoke in an authoritative manner. "I think Slim is our guy. Why else would he run from you that night in the casino if he was innocent?"

Wearily, I leaned back against the seat. My nausea had

returned, and I was worn out. "All we know about Slim is that he went to school with Smiley and that they both liked to play poker. If he has a motive for wanting Smiley dead, we still don't know what it is."

"How about Tina or the other woman on the set, Skye?" Josie asked. "Tina might have done away with him or helped Corey carry out the deed."

"I think that's unlikely. I can't picture her as a killer. And as for Skye—again, we don't have a motive."

"Could there be someone else from the set who we haven't considered?" Josie asked.

With a sigh, I reached for my phone and pressed a number in my contact section. "Desperate situations call for desperate measures."

"Who are you calling?" Josie wanted to know.

After one ring, a male voice came over the speaker and greeted us from my hands free. "Why, hello, Sally."

"You know my number too?" Seriously what didn't the man know about me?

"Of course," Jerry cooed. "You're my favorite local celebrity."

Josie's nostrils flared when she realized who it was. "I've got a couple of things to say to that piece of garbage."

"Is that the lovely Mrs. Sullivan?" Jerry asked sweetly. "How may I help you both today?"

"I want Angela Jones's phone number," I said. "And you're going to give it to me."

Jerry made a *tsk-tsk* sound. "That's privileged information, Mrs. Donovan. Besides, you've already been to see her. What else could you possibly need?"

Josie and I exchanged surprised glances. "How did you know that I went to see her?"

"You really should look around once in a while, my dear." Jerry suppressed a yawn. "I'm everywhere, remember."

"Gee, are we boring you?" Josie sneered.

"A little," he admitted. "I might be willing to give you Angela's phone number, Sally, but I need to know what's in it for me."

"You're lower than pond scum," Josie yelled. "If it wasn't for you writing all that trash about Sal and her bakery, we wouldn't even need to find Smiley's killer."

He snorted. "Now, I don't believe that for one second. Sally Donovan staying out of a murder investigation is like asking Dom Muccio to stay away from a cemetery."

Anger ignited in the bottom of my stomach. It was one thing for Jerry to make fun of me, but I drew the line when it came to my family. "It's the least you can do. Perhaps you've forgotten how you were almost killed while following me around?"

"That's right," Josie chimed in. "You owe Sal big time. Otherwise, karma's going to catch up with you soon."

"Oh, please," Jerry laughed. "I don't believe in all the fortune cookie malarkey."

"Come on," I pleaded. "After all the trouble you've caused, you owe me this much."

Jerry gave a little sigh on his end. "Well, since I am such a good guy, I suppose I could do you this one favor." He recited the number while I copied it into my phone. "But if you find out anything good, you have to promise to share it with me. Angela won't take my calls."

"Gee, I wonder why." I clicked off before he could say anything further. "Maybe he's turning over a new leaf."

"Forget it. Jerry Maroon is like gum on the bottom of your shoe," Josie declared. "Useless and disgusting. What do you want to talk to Angela about?"

I waited for her to pick up. "If Slim was a good friend of Smiley's, Angela must know him, right? And she'll give us his address."

"Then there's no need to call her," Josie said. "I'm sure that Brian would give it to—" She stopped abruptly.

I couldn't resist a chuckle. "What were you going to say?"

"Never mind."

After five rings, the phone was finally picked up. "Hello," Angela said cautiously.

Her low and husky voice forced me to think back to last night. Could it have been Angela who attacked me? I still didn't know for certain.

"Hello?" Impatience seeped into Angela's tone.

"Hi, Angela. This is Sally Donovan calling. We met the other day. How are you?"

Heavy breathing, similar to that of an obscene phone caller, filled my car. "You want to know how I am? I am tired of being harassed by reporters, police, and now you. I told you everything I knew. Now, stop bothering me!"

"Please wait!" I pleaded. "I just want to ask you one more thing. Do you know Slim Daniels, who also goes by Miles Merriweather?"

There was dead silence for several seconds. "Yeah, I know him," Angela admitted. "He was Jonas's best friend. Why are you asking about him?"

"Is there any way that he could have been involved with Jonas's death?"

Angela hesitated a bit too long. "Why would you think that Miles had anything to do with it?"

"We'd just like to talk to him," I said. "No one's been able to find him. It makes him look guilty, even if he isn't."

She was silent again. "I don't know why he would have been involved. They always got along great—like brothers. Hold on a second. I have his address in my phone somewhere."

I waited, listening as she mumbled to herself on the other end. "Here it is. He lives at 55 Westchester Lane in Buffalo. He travels a lot, on temporary jobs with TV stations. That's probably why you haven't been able to find him. I'm sure he must have talked to the police by now."

I started the engine while Josie punched Slim's address into Google Maps. "Does he have a gambling addiction like Jonas?"

She sounded surprised. "How the heck would I know? Jonas would tell me that he was meeting him at the casino sometimes, but I didn't keep track. If you're really serious about finding my husband's killer, maybe you should look at that so-called director of his show. Smiley knew that Corey was cheating on his wife. Now leave me alone. *Forever.*" She clicked off.

"Cripes," Josie mumbled. "Is there anyone who *didn't* know about the affair?"

"Jerry knows," I reminded her. "So now everyone knows."

Slim's house was located about ten minutes away from the high school. I pulled onto Westchester Drive and started looking for house number 55. "There has to be something—or someone—that we're overlooking."

The house was a small, light-blue ranch, perfectly landscaped with rose bushes and azaleas in full bloom out front.

We climbed the three steps leading to the wraparound porch and rang the bell. No answer.

Josie peered through the window. "It looks dark as tombs in there."

I rang the doorbell again, but no one came. I walked around the side of the house, with Josie following. There was a small fenced-in yard that contained a brick patio, some lawn chairs, a hammock, and gas barbecue. I peered into the side window of the garage. No car. "Looks like he's still not home."

Josie shrugged. "Well, at least we didn't waste a lot of time coming here."

We returned to my vehicle, and I was getting ready to pull away from the curb when my phone buzzed. Brian's name popped up, and I pressed the hands free. "Hi Brian."

"Sally, where are you?"

His tone was brisk and sharp, and I suspected I knew why. "Josie and I just left McKinstry High School." It was only a teeny white lie. We had been there earlier, after all. "Hey, did you know that Smiley was here a couple of weeks ago to talk to the students?"

There was a long, angry pause from the other end. When Brian spoke again, his voice was more reserved. "No, I didn't know. But I do seem to recall asking—or should I say—telling you to lie low since you are in danger again. Do you ever listen to me?"

"Brian, I—"

"Save it," he interrupted. "Where are you now?"

I conveniently skipped over the part about visiting Slim's house. "On our way home."

"Really, Brian," Josie scolded. "Sal needs to find out who killed Smiley because she *is* in danger. We don't sit back and wait around for others to take care of our problems. We're all about action."

She wasn't helping the situation any. "Josie doesn't mean that you aren't taking care of things," I explained. "She just means that—"

"Yeah, I know what she means," Brian said curtly. "All right, let's have it. What else did you learn during your visit to the school?"

I shifted in my seat. "We found out that Smiley brought a friend with him when he visited, and it was none other than Slim

Daniels. It seems that they both went to McKinstry High and were best friends. They even had the same slogans in their yearbook."

"And they were both on the school's playing card team," Josie added.

"High schools have playing card teams?" Brian sounded amazed. "Jeez, I must have gone to school during the stone age. We didn't even have football."

"McKinstry is one of the top schools in the Buffalo area," I explained. "From what I've heard, they offer a lot of activities other schools don't."

Brian cleared his throat. "Okay, getting back to the subject at hand. I just spoke to Angela Jones a few minutes ago, and she practically bit my head off. She wasn't happy about receiving a phone call from Nancy Drew and her twin."

"Nancy didn't have a twin," Josie volunteered. "But her friends, George and Bess, were cousins. I read all those books as a kid and—"

"Whatever!" Brian shouted. "Do not contact that woman again, Sally. She could try to charge you with harassment."

"We only called her because we wanted Slim's address and knew that you wouldn't give it to us." Too late, Josie clasped a hand over her mouth.

I had a strong urge to bang my head against the steering wheel. "Thanks for that, Jos."

"I don't believe this," Brian muttered. "You were almost attacked, but you're back at it, bothering all the murder suspects and putting yourself in plain view, all for nothing."

"It wasn't for nothing," I said. "We did manage to get Slim's phone number while we were at the school. Would you like it?"

Brian cleared his throat. "That won't be necessary. I have Slim's number. In fact, let me save you the trouble before you drive out to his house, because I know that's where you're headed. He's here."

"Excuse me?"

He enunciated each word carefully. "Slim. Is. At. The. Station. And before you even try to ask, no, you cannot question him."

"I wasn't going to ask," I lied.

"Sally, I wasn't born yesterday," Brian said. "I know you

and your sidekick a little too well."

Josie winked at me. "I've been called worse things."

"Come on, Brian," I pleaded. "The man ran away from me at the casino. He's clearly hiding something."

"Maybe he spotted that death hex on your head. That would scare off anyone." He sighed. "Look, I can't have you in the interrogation room when I question him. Do I have to remind you that you're not a police officer?"

"Will you at least let me know what you find out?" I asked eagerly.

Brian ignored my question. "Oh, and one more thing. Jerry Maroon announced in his latest gossip column this morning that Corey Whitaker's wife knew about his affair with Tina. Seems that she threw him out of the house."

"How does he always get this information before anyone else?" I asked.

"Darned if I know," Brian said. "But I'm starting to think we should hire him on the police force. Talk to you soon."

"Brian, wait!"

It was too late. He'd already clicked off.

Josie watched me thoughtfully. "What now?"

"Well, all I know is that I'm not sitting around waiting for Brian to call me." I stared the engine.

"If he even bothers to call," Josie added.

I made a U-turn on the street. "Colwestern Police Station, here we come."

She grinned and leaned back in her seat. "You never disappoint, Sal."

Twenty minutes later, we walked into the station. Al Farley, the man behind the front counter, had been with the department for as long as I could remember. He took one look at us and groaned.

"You two *again*? Maybe you ladies want to take up permanent residence here," he chortled.

"Real funny," Josie murmured.

"Brian's in the interrogation room," Al said to me. "Is he expecting you?"

"Yes," I lied. "Could you tell him that we're here?"

Al heaved himself out of his comfortable chair and started down the hallway. "Hang on a second."

After he had disappeared, a woman entered the station.

She was wearing a beige raincoat and hood that partially hid her face. When she removed the hood, my heart skipped a beat. She turned her head in my direction, and when our gazes met, recognition registered in her eyes. She started to walk toward us.

"Holy cow," Josie murmured under her breath. "What are you doing here?"

Skye's dark eyes shifted back and forth between us. "I need to tell Detective Jenkins something," she whispered. "Something about Smiley's killer."

CHAPTER EIGHTEEN

My heart was racing with excitement, but I tried to remain calm. "Why don't we sit down and wait for him." I motioned to a nearby bench.

Skye shook her head. "Thanks, but I think I'll stand."

"What exactly did you want to tell Brian—er, Detective Jenkins?" I asked.

She swallowed hard. "The day that Smiley was killed, I forgot my phone charger in your bakery. I came back for it after the taping finished."

My eyebrows drew together. "I don't remember seeing you."

Skye twisted her hands together. "That's because I never came inside. Smiley was talking to someone in front of your bakery."

Josie sucked in a breath. "Who was it?"

"A woman," Skye said. "But I couldn't get a good look at her face. She was wearing a pink sweatshirt and had the hood pulled over her head. They were standing really close together, and holding hands. After a few seconds, they both went inside your bakery. I was starting to feel real uncomfortable at this point, so I left. Neither one of them saw me."

"This is very important," I said. "What do you remember about the woman? Was she thin or heavyset? Short? Tall?"

Skye shrugged. "I really didn't pay much attention. I just assumed it was a woman because of the pink sweatshirt. Like I said, I couldn't see her face."

"Sally, what are you doing here?" an irritated voice asked from behind me.

I turned to see Brian standing there, hands on his hips. He did not look happy.

Gulp. I raised my hand. "Brian, it's not what you think—"

"Save it," he interrupted. "I thought I told you not to come down here."

Skye looked confused. "Are you helping the police with the investigation?"

"Yes, I am," I replied, with a careful eye on Brian.

Brian let out a loud snort. "That's debatable."

I chose to ignore his disparaging remark. "Brian, we need to talk after you're finished questioning your suspect."

"Then why did you tell Al to come and interrupt me?" Brian asked.

Because I wanted to know what was going on, but I couldn't tell him that. "I only said that—"

Josie nudged me. "Sal, look!"

I followed Josie's gaze and saw Skye sneaking towards the exit. "Wait!" I shouted and hurried after her. Skye had a trapped looked in her eyes that reminded me of a caged animal. I placed a gentle hand on her arm. "Please, Skye. You have to tell Brian what you saw."

Brian approached us. "It's okay, Skye. What did you want to tell me?"

Skye remained stoic, so I jumped in. "She saw a woman talking outside of my bakery with Smiley, shortly before he was killed."

Brian cut his eyes to Skye. "Would you mind waiting for me in my office? It's the second door on the right."

Skye hesitated for a moment then nodded. "All right."

We watched as she walked away and disappeared into the room he'd indicated.

"Your own office, huh?" Josie grinned. "You've really moved up in the world, Brian."

Color rose in Brian's cheeks. "Sally, I would appreciate it if you and your friend would leave now. You're both disasters waiting to happen."

I'd had enough of his jabs. "Oh, come off it. Yes, I know that I'm a murder magnet in your eyes, Brian, but please try to see this from my point of view. I'm only trying to help. Every day that this case goes unsolved costs me a ton of money."

"What about me?" Josie piped in. "I've got a kid looking at colleges."

Brian's shoulders slumped forward, as if in defeat. "Look, I know you're only trying to help, but I don't want to see anything happen to either one of you. At this point, I don't know any more than you do. Yes, I realize that your bakery is where the murder took place, and I feel bad about that, but my job is to find Smiley's killer. I can't be worrying about how many cookies you didn't sell and if your grandmother and Nicoletta make it to Italy."

Heat rose into my face. "I realize it may not matter to you, but I'd like to see my grandmother get her trip to Italy. Her happiness means the world to me. And I understand that you aren't concerned about my bakery."

"Even though you frequent it enough," Josie put in.

I was on a roll now. "All things considered, Brian, you have to admit that over the years, I've been more of a help than a hindrance to you. *Especially* last summer."

Brian lowered his gaze to the floor and didn't answer right away. I knew that I had touched a nerve. It wasn't my intention to embarrass him in front of Josie with the painful memory, but he did owe me.

Last August, Brian had been in danger of losing his job on the police force and serving a prison sentence for the murder of a former girlfriend. He'd asked me to help him, and I never thought twice about doing so. I'd known all along that he wasn't guilty of the crime, but that wasn't the point. Friends are supposed to help one another. We'd both almost lost our lives in an attempt to prove his innocence.

"You're right," he said slowly. "I'll never forget what you did for me, Sally. If Slim doesn't have any objection, you can come in while I finish questioning him. But I don't want to hear a peep out of you."

"Me too?" Josie asked hopefully.

Brian shook his head. "Wait out in the hall, please."

"I could keep Skye company," Josie volunteered.

"That won't be necessary," he said.

Josie looked disappointed but did as Brian asked. He led me to the door of the interrogation room, then held up a finger for me to wait while he went inside. The murmur of quiet voices could be heard, and a minute later, he opened the door and ushered me inside.

"Sally, you remember Slim Daniels," Brian said by way of introduction. He gestured at a chair in the corner of the room. "Slim has no problem with you staying. Sit over there, please."

Slim nodded at me. "I had nothing to do with Jonas's

murder."

Brian reached forward and turned a recording device on. "Okay, let's continue, Mr. Daniels. As you were saying before—"

Slim jumped up suddenly. The action was so unexpected that Brian reached for his gun. "Smiley was a friend. My best friend, in fact. We go back a long way, since we were kids."

"Please sit back down," Brian said quietly.

Slim jabbed a finger in my direction. "You want to know the real reason I said you could come in? Because I have nothing to hide, I swear."

"Then why did you run from me at the casino?" I asked.

He shrugged and stared over at Brian. "I got spooked when I saw you, and the detective here in the casino. It felt like you both were in cahoots, or something. I kind of freaked and took off. That's why I take temporary jobs on sets. I can't stay in the same place for very long."

Brian shook his head at me. "What did I tell you about keeping quiet?" He turned back to Slim. "The police went to your house, and you deliberately stayed away."

"It was all a misunderstanding," he protested.

I wasn't buying it, and from the look on Brian's face, neither was he. We waited for the man to go on.

With a sigh, Slim hung his head and placed his hands on the table. "Okay, here's the truth. I was afraid that my, shall we say—extracurricular activities—would come out. I've got a fiancé who doesn't know anything about my poker playing, and I'd like to keep it that way."

I still couldn't be positive that he was telling the truth. "Someone tried to abduct me behind my bakery the other night. Would you know anything about that?"

He shook his head. "No way. I told you that I wasn't involved in this mess. I didn't know anyone on the set of *Senior Moments* except for Smiley. He's the one who got me the job. It might be a temporary gig, but they pay the bills."

"When was the last time you saw Smiley?" Brian wanted to know.

Slim seemed surprised by the question. "When I left the bakery, after the taping finished. It was around five o'clock. Corey thanked me and said that if they got back to the area again, he'd look me up."

"You didn't happen to come back to the bakery and see

Smiley talking outside with a woman?" I asked.

Brian narrowed his eyes at me. "Whoops," I said. "Sorry."

Slim shook his head. "Nope. And I don't believe Smiley was fooling around with that Tatiana gal on set."

"Tina," Brian said patiently. "Her name is Tina."

"Yeah, that's it," Slim agreed. "Smiley may have had a gambling problem, but he wasn't cheating on his wife. They weren't even divorced yet."

"Where did you hear that Smiley was fooling around with Tina?" This came from Brian.

Slim shrugged. "One of the guys on the set was talking about Tina being, you know, easy and all. He implied that she was sleeping with someone from the show, so I figured he meant Smiley."

"Did you see Smiley often?" I asked.

Brian threw up his hands but allowed Slim to answer my question.

Slim hesitated. "He'd come by every month or so. Jonas liked the area—he grew up here. That doesn't make me a killer."

"Did he owe you money?" Brian asked. "From what I've heard, he owed everyone."

"No," Slim said through tight lips. "I already told you I didn't kill him. Maybe it was the person who was sending him the notes."

"What notes?" Then I remembered what Angela had said about Smiley's fan mail.

Slim leaned back in his chair. "He'd get threatening notes once in a while. At first, he just figured that they were from old men who didn't make it on the show or elderly women who complained the man of their dreams had turned out to be a real dud."

Like Earl.

"But it all seemed harmless until last week," Slim continued.

Brian leaned forward. "Go on."

Slim scratched his head. "I didn't see the note, but Smiley called me and told me about it. I could tell by his tone he was rattled."

"What did it say?" I asked.

He frowned. "Something along the lines of, 'you can run,

but you'll never escape what you did. And I'll make sure that you pay.'"

"What does that mean?" Brian looked baffled.

The truth hit me like a slap to the face. "Oh my God."

Both men looked over at me.

"I can't be positive," I admitted, "but remember how you said that Smiley killed someone in an accident a few years ago?"

"He didn't set out to hurt anyone," Slim said quickly. "Jonas felt awful about it."

I stared at him in disbelief. "He took another person's life because he was high. Being sorry won't bring them back. Did you ever find out the person's name, Brian? It was a woman, correct?"

"Her name was Priscilla," Slim volunteered. "I can't remember the last name. Wheatley, maybe?"

There was a knock on the door. Brian pinched his nose between his thumb and forefinger then slowly rose to his feet and opened it. Josie almost fell into the room.

"What are you doing here?" he said in an exasperated tone. "I thought I told you to wait in the hall."

The freckles stood out on Josie's pale face. "Skye's gone," She whispered.

"Where? Why would she leave?" Brian asked.

Josie swallowed nervously. "She said it was a mistake to come here."

CHAPTER NINETEEN

"What are you looking for, Sal?" Josie asked.

I typed Skye Crandall's name into the Google search window of my laptop. "I want to see if I can find out anything about Skye. Maybe there's something that will connect her with Smiley."

Josie leaned against one of the tables in the storefront. "I don't get it. She came out of Brian's office, and I tried to make small talk with her. We talked about nothing of real importance. The weather, what a wardrobe person does, blah blah. Then, all of a sudden, she burst into tears and runs out the door. Do you think Smiley or someone on the set attacked her?"

"Anything's possible." The results of my search turned up only one Skye Crandall. She was fifty years old and lived in California. Yeah, definitely not her. "Do you think Crandall might not be her real name?"

Josie shrugged. "I guess, but not everyone's on Google, are they?"

"Almost everyone," I joked. "Except maybe for Cookie."

Josie picked up the broom and resumed sweeping the floor. "I counted six customers in here today. Hey, we're improving."

I moved away from the screen and rubbed my eyes. "I know. It's beyond frustrating."

"This is crazy, Sal." She leaned on the broom. "We have to do something."

"It's going to have to wait until tomorrow." I went to the sink for a glass of water. "Right now, I'm too tired to think straight."

Josie dumped the contents of the dustpan into the garbage. "Do you want me to lock up?"

"No, you go ahead and take off. At least I don't have to

worry about rush hour traffic anymore."

She disappeared into the kitchen and a minute later returned, her purse and car keys in hand. "Don't worry, Sal. You'll figure it out. I have complete faith in you."

"Thanks, but Smiley's murder has really got me confused. I feel like there's some angle I've missed."

"A motive?" Josie suggested. "Or maybe a suspect?"

I positioned my fingers on the laptop's keyboard. "There's certainly plenty of both to go around. I think Skye knows more than she's letting on."

"I feel like everyone involved in this murder knows more than they're letting on," Josie admitted. "But I don't want you staying here by yourself. It's far too dangerous. Is Mike coming to take you home?"

"I wish," I said glumly. "He had an emergency roof repair job to take care of. Cookie's over at my parents with Grandma. Dad and Mom are hosting a wake at the funeral home tonight."

Josie chuckled. "That must have made your father happy."

"Well, you know Dad. Nothing like a good funeral to cheer him up."

"I still don't want you going anywhere alone." Josie's eyes were anxious. "I'll wait for you."

"It's okay. Gianna's already thought of that. She's going to meet me here when she gets done with work. It shouldn't be too long."

Josie's face relaxed. "Okay. Have a good night then and I'll see you in the morning." She waved and went out the front door, locking it behind her.

I watched as she got into her minivan, which she'd left parked at the curb today. We usually tried to keep those spaces available for customers, but there was no need to today. Something had to change, and soon.

With a sigh, I turned my attention back to the laptop and tried to focus, remembering the conversation I'd had with Brian after finding Smiley's body. He'd told Josie and me how Smiley had killed one woman—Priscilla—and paralyzed another. I'd already checked out everything about Smiley online but could find no mention of the accident. Brian had told me earlier to leave the search to him. He'd said that I wouldn't be able to find out any details because it had all been hushed up. Smiley had paid off the families so that he could "make it all go away."

Who else did I know that always had the dirt on everyone? This was a no brainer. I picked up my phone and punched in a number. The phone rang twice before I heard Jerry's cheery voice.

"Twice in one day, Mrs. Donovan? To what do I owe this honor?"

"I need another favor."

Jerry clucked his tongue against the roof of his mouth. "I believe that you're fresh out of favors. Everything has its price, my dear. What are you going to do for me?"

What a slime. "Look, you've practically closed down my business with that article you wrote. So, I don't think that you should be asking me for anything."

To my surprise, he sounded almost regretful. "I realize that was unfortunate, but it's my job to present the facts to the public."

"What a load of bull," I spat out. "Those weren't facts. I'm not a death magnet. And now, with the help of your poisoned pen, someone's trying to kill me. You could keep spewing lies or do the right thing and help me."

There was a long pause. "All right, what did you need?"

"What can you tell me about the woman Smiley killed three years ago?"

"Not much," Jerry confessed. "There were two women involved in the accident."

Jerry Maroon didn't have all the details. What the heck was this world coming to? "I need to know their names."

"Hang on a second—let me check something I found the other day." I heard the click clack of his keyboard, and then he giggled like a schoolgirl. "Aha! Here it is. The deceased's name was Priscilla Wheaton, and Annie Rather is the woman who was paralyzed. Both of them were from the Buffalo area."

"Do you have contact information for them?" I pressed.

He let out a snicker. "Jeez, I'm good, but I'm not God. Let me see what else I can dig up. It might take me a day or two, but I'll find out all the gory details. And then we'll talk about ways you can help my next budding career move."

"What are you talking about?"

"I'm thinking about running for mayor," Jerry continued. "Once the bakery's business bounces back, I think you'd be a great contact to help me get votes. You could even print messages in your fortune cookies that say, '*Your life will be merry, if you just vote for Jerry.*'"

My stomach twisted at his words. It felt like I was making a deal with the devil. "Okay, we'll see," I lied. Jerry's name was never going to make it inside my fortune cookies. "Now, answer me one question, please. How are you always the first person to get dirt on someone?"

He laughed. "I never divulge my secrets. Ciao, Mrs. Donovan." With that, he was gone.

My phone pinged with a message from Gianna. *Sorry, Sal, I'm running late. I should be there within an hour. Please don't leave without me!*

Sighing, I typed both women's names into the laptop. There was nothing on Annie, but I did find an obituary for Priscilla. It was short and to the point.

Priscilla Wheaton, wife of Charles Wheaton, died suddenly on Monday, March 25. Services will be private and held at the convenience of the family. Monetary donations for her burial can be made directly to the Phibbins Mortuary Home.

Holy cow. Phibbins Mortuary had been owned by Eddie Phibbins, a local funeral director who was a good friend of my father's. He was murdered last year, and Dad had pleaded with me to help find his killer. Dad had actually been the one to discover Eddie's body, which had been found in—of all places—one of Eddie's caskets.

My father now owned the same funeral home.

With trembling hands, I called my father. He picked up after five rings, with his usual rehearsed speech. He couldn't just say, "Hello. Muccio Mortuary." That was too simple.

"It's a great day at Muccio Mortuary. How can we service you or your loved ones today? This is Domenic Muccio, proprietor, renowned author, blogger, and all-around—"

"Dad!" I interrupted. "This is urgent. Do you have records for all of the past services that Eddie Phibbins conducted?"

"Of course," my father replied. "Eddie's rule was to keep files on hand for at least seven years. And you know my rule."

"Yes." Never throw anything away. I half expected to see my father on *Hoarders* one day. My heart continued to thump against the wall of my chest. "Can you find the file for a Priscilla

Wheaton and tell me the names of her relatives?"

"Hmm. Well, your mother is in the viewing room, making sure everything's going according to plan with the service. Tell you what. Give me ten minutes to call you back, baby girl."

He clicked off before I could reply. I would have preferred to wait, but there was a knock on my front door. I put the phone down and glanced at my watch. Four fifty-five. Technically, we were still open, and I needed every sale I could get my hands on. I peeked through the slits in the window blind and saw Skye waving frantically at me.

"Please, I need to talk to you!" she shouted through the glass. "Right away!""

With sickening dread, I unlocked the door, and she rushed inside. Skye was sobbing uncontrollably, and I tried to console her. "What's wrong? And what happened to you at the police station? Why didn't you wait for Detective Jenkins?"

"I don't know," she faltered. "He kind of scares me. He seemed so angry."

"He's always like that—well, around me, anyway," I said. "Brian would never do anything to hurt you."

Skye reached a gloved hand into her coat pocket. The day had turned damp and chilly, but it seemed odd for to be wearing gloves in May. "I remembered something about the woman I saw Smiley with and thought you and your friend would want to know. Josie, right?"

"Josie went home, but you can tell me." I pointed to the table where I'd been sitting earlier. "Have a seat."

Skye obeyed and took the chair I'd vacated earlier. "I'm glad you came to see me, but you should really be talking to the police first."

"Please, can't you tell the detective for me?" she begged. "I freeze up around him."

"You're going to have to talk to him eventually," I said. "Can I do anything else to help?"

She shot me a grateful smile. "Remember when I told you that I saw Smiley with a woman outside of your bakery?"

"Yes, of course." I leaned forward eagerly.

Skye twisted her hands in her lap. "The woman was tall, like Smiley. And when she turned around, her hood was pushed back a little. I only saw her hair for a split second, before she turned around, but I'm almost positive she was blonde. Not dirty blonde, but kind of like a whitish blonde. Does that help?"

Holy cow. The woman must have been Angela. Why had she been in town to see Smiley if they were on the verge of a divorce? It sounded like they'd both accepted the fate of their marriage and decided to move on.

A chill ran down my spine. Had Angela been the one to do her husband in? Why would she have killed him in such a gruesome manner? I already knew the answer. A million dollars was a lot of money.

Skye waved a hand in front of my face. "Are you okay?"

"Sure." I blinked. "Just fine."

She watched me carefully. "You know who killed him, don't you?"

"I don't have concrete proof, but this is a good tip. Thank you. I'll let Brian know right away."

She shifted in her seat. "Could I trouble you for a glass of water?"

"Of course." I rose from my chair. "Would you rather have something else, like coffee? And maybe a cookie to go with it?"

Skye's gaze wandered over to the display case. "No thanks. They look terrific, but I need to watch myself. Once I start eating sweets, I can't stop."

"Yes, I have the same problem. I'll go grab your water." I couldn't help but think that there was something pathetic and sad about Skye, as if a halo of depression surrounded her. When I went into the back room to fill a glass from the sink, my phone buzzed. I fished it out of my pocket and pressed *Accept Call*. "Hi, Dad."

"Baby girl, I've got that information you wanted," he said. "Priscilla Wheaton died three years and two months ago in an automobile accident. Fortunately, Eddie took meticulous notes on every person who was brought into the funeral home. I like to think that I'm following in his footsteps. Anyway, Priscilla's husband Charlie and her parents, Ron and Elizabeth Crandall, were so grief stricken that they couldn't cope with a public viewing. They felt that it would be better to—"

A light bulb switched on in my brain. "Whoa. Hang on a second. Did you say that her parents last name was Crandall?"

"That's right," Dad said. "Why? Do you know them?"

The blood in my veins quickly turned to icicles. Pieces were starting to fit together, and I didn't like the puzzle reveal. "Are there any other relatives mentioned?"

"Nope," Dad said. "Those are the only names that Eddie wrote down. What's going on, Sal? This has to do with Smiley's murder, right?"

"Thanks for the information, Dad, but I don't have time to explain now. Can we talk about it later?"

"Sure," he replied. "Are you and Mike coming to dinner?"

"Mike's working late, but I'll be there."

"Great. Rosa's making lasagna." He sounded excited, and I could picture a lopsided grin on his round, cherubic face. "Bring some fortune cookies with you, Sal. I'm feeling lucky."

I was glad that someone felt lucky because all I had was a dreadful lump in the bottom of my stomach. Thanks to my father's discovery, I was convinced there was a murderer in my storefront. I pressed the button for Brian's cell as I heard the silver bells jingle on my front door. Oh no. Skye had bolted again. What if we couldn't find her this time? Perhaps she'd overheard my conversation.

"Skye?" I called out.

There was no answer.

"Shoot." Maybe I could get her license plate before she left. As I hurried through the door into the storefront, something connected with the back of my head. A numbing pain consumed me, and stars danced before my eyes. With a cry, I slumped to the floor and was surrounded by inky blackness.

CHAPTER TWENTY

A tugging on my wrists awakened me. When I opened my eyes, the bright light from the ceiling shone down on my face and nearly split my head in two. I turned in the direction of my attacker.

Skye was busy fastening my hands together with what looked like cut-off ties from my aprons. I began to struggle and was rewarded with a stinging slap to the side of my face. My head snapped back at the sudden action, and tears sprang to my eyes.

"Don't try anything," she warned. "Unless you want to go the same way as Smiley."

Fear consumed me as I watched her tying my wrists, whistling under her breath as she worked. I glanced towards the window and tried to judge what time it was, but the blinds were closed, and I had no idea. I couldn't have been unconscious long if Skye was still in the process of tying me up. My laptop lay a few feet away from me with its shattered screen. Skye didn't have a rolling pin this time, but she'd still managed to get the job done.

"Why didn't you kill me already?" My voice trembled. "You didn't let Smiley live, so why me?"

My question was rewarded with an extra tug on the ties, making me wince in pain. "Because when I came here, I didn't know if you'd figured everything out. You left the page on your laptop open to my sister's obituary. Not very smart. So, I don't have any choice but to get rid of you."

"I don't know what you're talking about," I lied.

Skye scoffed. "Please don't insult my intelligence. I should have taken care of you the other night in the rain and saved myself all this trouble. Unlike the fortune cookies, your luck has run out."

The muscles on her arms bulged as she wrapped the ties around my wrists. She'd removed her gloves, and there was a large Band-Aid over her right thumb, which must have been slowing her down. Now I knew the reason for the gloves. I remembered the brute force she'd used on me the other night, when it seemed that my attacker had to be a man. But I had been wrong—dead wrong.

Satisfied with her job, Skye stood and began pacing around the table. "Look, I don't enjoy killing people. Except for Smiley, that is. He had it coming. I just have to figure out how to get rid of you without any witnesses around. We'll have to wait until it's dark, and then I'll smuggle you out through the alley to my car. Who were you on the phone with in the back room? I heard you mention my last name. Does someone know that I'm here? You'd better tell me the truth."

No one knows. How I wished someone did know Skye were here. I debated for a second about what to say. If I told her no one, she might not waste any time beating me to death like she'd done with Smiley, or worse. "My father."

Skye muttered a curse word under her breath. "All right, on your feet. We have to leave now."

My head ached, and it was difficult to think straight. "Where are we going?"

"Where do you think?" she snapped. "To a party? I'll have to put you in my trunk." A broad grin spread across her face. "Maybe I'll leave you there for a couple of days. That would take care of the problem nicely. Then I'll dump your body in the nearest river."

I reminded myself to try and stay calm. *Deep breaths, Sal.* "It's not too late," I said. "Turn yourself in. You can get some help."

Her dark eyes scanned me up and down, and I watched as her expression turned to one of hate. "Help for what? There's nothing wrong with me. That scum of the earth got exactly what he deserved. He killed my sister, and no one even cared! Can you believe it? Smiley didn't even do any jail time. And to top it all off, Priscilla's loser husband decided to settle out of court for the money. Do you know how that made me feel? It killed my parents. They both passed away—six months apart. Say what you want, but I know they died of broken hearts."

"I'm sorry."

Skye waved a hand dismissively in the air. "Oh please. You don't care. No one does. It's like her life didn't matter to anyone." She picked up a butcher knife from the table and fingered the edge carefully. "But Priscilla mattered to me. And I promised her that he would pay—someday."

Cold, stark fear lodged itself in my throat, and I couldn't breathe. The woman was clearly unhinged. There was nothing I could do except keep her talking in hope that help might arrive soon. "You never saw Smiley and Angela outside of my bakery. It was a lie to throw me off the track."

She tossed back her long black hair and rewarded me with a smile. "Correct. I'd seen pictures of Smiley and his wife online and figured that she was the most likely person to blame. Then I read an article from your local paper that said she was inheriting a life insurance policy for a million dollars, so she seemed like the perfect suspect."

I mumbled a curse word in my head. *Thank you, Jerry Maroon.*

Skye continued. "I majored in fashion merchandising, so I've been working temporary jobs until I could find something permanent. When the employment agency told me there was an opening on the shoot because the regular wardrobe woman was sick, I jumped at the chance. You don't know how long I've been waiting for this opportunity."

Three years, I was betting. "How did you get back into my bakery that day?"

"I stole your keys." Skye's eyes shone with excitement. "They were sitting there in plain view on the counter. Then, I waited down the street for you and Smiley to leave. I figured once I killed him, I could plant some evidence in the bakery to make it look like you did it. But when you left, he was still sitting out front in his car. It was too good to be true. So, I entered the bakery through the back door."

She paused and I fearfully waited for her to go on.

Skye laughed. "Smiley the loser had nowhere to go. I ran over and rapped on his window, saying that I'd lost my purse, and asked if he'd come back and help me look for it. When he asked how I got inside, I said that you must have forgotten to lock the back door, and the idiot believed me."

"And that's when you told him who you were."

She shook her head. "No, I'm not into dramatics. I had nothing to say to that creep. All I felt was rage whenever I looked at him. So, I waited until he had his back to me and then cracked the rolling pin onto his skull as hard as I could. He went down like a sack of potatoes." Her face took on a faraway look. "Once I started, I couldn't stop."

Bile rose in the back of my throat. Skye's hands began to shake as she dropped the butcher knife back on the table. She exhaled sharply. "I'm not sorry I did it. Only that you found out."

I struggled with the ties around my wrists but couldn't get them to budge.

Skye came out of her trance and laughed at me. "Forget it. A scrawny little thing like you can't get out of those, unless you're Wonder Woman in disguise." She picked up the laptop from the floor. "Looks like I'll have to knock you out and carry you to my car."

As she started towards me, a loud tapping sounded on the front door. Skye jumped in surprise. She quickly picked up the knife and held it in under my nose in warning. "If you say anything, I swear I'll gut you like a fish."

I waited in fearful silence, praying the person wouldn't leave. Skye wasted no time in stuffing part of the apron in my mouth until I feared I might gag. After a few seconds, the knock came again.

"Oh, Mrs. Donovan," a male voice sang out. "Let me in before I huff and puff and blow your bakery down."

Skye scrunched her eyebrows together in confusion. "Who's that freak?"

With a mouthful of cloth, I was unable to answer, but knew the voice belonged to Jerry.

"Come on, Sally. Talk to me." Jerry sounded wounded. "I've done a lot of favors for you today, so you need to tell me what you know about Smiley's killer. You're not playing fair here."

The silence in my bakery was deafening as we waited for what felt like an eternity, Finally, Jerry spoke again. "Okay, I'll be back."

My heart sank as his footsteps faded away. Jerry had been my last hope. I debated making a run for the door, but Skye would stop me, and who knew what she would do then.

Skye cautiously approached the front window and peered out between the blinds. Satisfied, she exhaled and turned back to me. "Don't try anything funny. You'll only die sooner. Understand?"

I gave a quick nod as Skye dragged me to my feet and pushed me ahead of her towards the kitchen. "Move. We're going out the back door."

With no choice, I stumbled ahead of her, hoping for a chance to break away. All I needed was a few split seconds. It wouldn't be easy with my wrists tied in front of me, but I had to try.

When we reached the back door, Skye peeked out into the alley, looking both ways. Once she was satisfied there was no one around, she pushed me towards her vehicle and lifted the trunk. "Get in."

I didn't move.

"Don't push me," she spat out. "Get in, or I'll throw you in."

Jerry's head popped up from the other side of Skye's car. He pointed a pistol at her. "Sorry to interrupt, but I think that would be a very bad idea." He moved around the back of the car, heading towards us.

Quick as a flash, Skye removed the knife from her pocket and held it against my throat. "Try anything, and she's dead."

Sirens wailed in the distance—the most beautiful sound I'd ever heard. Skye shrieked when she realized what was happening and pushed me into Jerry. She jumped into the driver's seat, turned the key in the ignition and throttled the engine. The tires began to spin, sending up clouds of dust through the air as Skye zoomed through the alley. Within seconds, her car was surrounded by two police cruisers and Brian's unmarked vehicle. Skye bolted from the car and tried to make a run for it. One of the officers ran after her and quickly tackled her. She landed face down on the ground.

Jerry removed my gag and began to untie my wrists. "Are you okay?" he asked.

"I think so," I said shakily. "Thanks for coming to my rescue."

He rewarded me with a goofy grin. "Hey, turnabout is fair play, right?"

Brian rushed over to us. "Are you all right, Sally?"

"Yes, I'm fine."

Brian waved Jerry off and used a pocketknife to cut the ties around my wrists. He shook his head. "Like I said before, trouble follows you everywhere. I'm glad that Jerry called us, and we were able to get here in time."

"How did you know we were inside the bakery?" I asked.

Jerry shot me a smug look. "Well, I have to confess that I was hanging around, waiting until your brute of a partner left the bakery. That woman scares me. Anyway, I saw the brunette go into your building. After a few minutes, I decided that I'd waited long enough. I went to the window and tried to peek inside. One of the blinds was broken, and I was able to see movement on the other side, but I couldn't tell who it was. When no one answered the door, I figured you might be in trouble, so I took a chance and called 9-1-1."

"You can really be a decent guy when you want to be."

"Well, don't let it get out," Jerry said. "It would ruin my reputation."

I was so grateful to be alive that I hugged him. "Thank you for saving my life. And I'm so glad you didn't have to use the gun."

He laughed. "Oh, this thing? It's not real."

I gasped. "What?"

Jerry smiled and twirled the gun around his finger like he was in an old Western movie. "It's only a water pistol."

* * *

Four days later, I placed my sleeping daughter in the crib my parents kept upstairs for their grandchildren. For a long moment, I stood there, watching my little angel. I sent a silent prayer of thanks above as I placed a hand over my stomach. More than ever, I had so many things to be grateful for.

The noisy racquet from downstairs caught my attention, and I smiled to myself. It was such beautiful noise—the sound of family. Sure, my parents were a bit odd and liked to march to the beat of their own drummer, but I could only appreciate them more after what had happened earlier in the week.

I covered Cookie with one of Grandma Rosa's handmade quilts and blew her a kiss. When I closed the door to the bedroom, my mother's voice drifted up the stairs. "Sal? Where are you? You're going to miss the start of the show, sweetie."

I started slowly down the stairs. The wallop from Skye resulted in a mild concussion, but there had been no lingering issues. Business at the bakery had returned to its normal volume, and even Jerry had paid our cookies a compliment in his latest article. And to think that some people didn't believe in miracles.

My entire family, Mrs. Gavelli, and Josie were all gathered in the living room to watch the latest episode of *Senior Moments*. Rumors were circulating that the show would continue next season with a new host to take Smiley's place. I sat down next to Mike on the couch and helped myself to a piece of cheesecake.

He leaned over and kissed me on the cheek. "Feeling okay, princess?"

"Never better." We exchanged a knowing glance as his arm went around my shoulders.

Gianna, seated on the floor with Alex, looked up and winked at me. "Once, again, Sally Muccio Donovan got her man—I mean, woman."

My mother was sitting on Dad's lap in the recliner and made a *tsk-tsk* sound. "I'm just glad that you're okay, sweetheart. That woman needs serious psychological help. I hope she gets some in prison."

"You'll have to testify when the case comes to trial," Gianna reminded me as Johnny brought her a glass of iced tea. She leaned over to kiss him as he flopped down next to her and Alex on the rug.

"Yeah, I figured, but it's not the first time." I could only hope that it might be the last, though.

"Humph." Mrs. Gavelli narrowed her eyes at me from across the room. "It good that you get this solved. Now, Rosa and I go Italy and have fun."

My father finished his piece of cheesecake and set his empty plate on the coffee table. "When do you leave, old lady? It can't be soon enough."

At that moment, my grandmother came into the room with a plate of Italian cheeses and crackers and set them on the coffee table. "We will not be going for three more months."

"I only wish it was sooner." Dad raised a glass of wine in salute. "Sorry, Rosa. Nothing against you, but the neighborhood is going to be nice and quiet for ten whole days. I'll drink to that."

Mrs. Gavelli shook her fist at him. "Why don't you climb in coffin and forget to get out?"

My father took a sip of his drink while he considered her question. "Hey, I almost did that once. It was so comfortable that

I didn't want to get out."

"Listen to both of you," Grandma Rosa scolded. "Such *pazzas*."

"Yeah, there's plenty of crazy in this room," Mike observed.

"Hey, Sal." Josie was sitting next to Mrs. Gavelli. "It's nice to see that you've got some color back in your face. You never did tell me what the doctor said."

I glanced over at Mike, who winked at me in return. It seemed like the perfect time to share our wonderful news. "Well, it looks like I'm pregnant."

"Oh my God!" my mother shrieked. She jumped off my father's lap and hurried across the room to throw her arms around me. Josie and Gianna followed. "Another grandchild! This is the best news ever!"

Josie looked confused. "I'm so happy for you guys. But I thought you said the test was negative?"

"It was, but the doctor insisted on doing some bloodwork," I explained. "He said that I had all the symptoms and the previous test may have been defective. It's rare, but can happen sometimes."

"When are you due, sweetheart?" my mother asked excitedly.

"Next January."

Johnny's mouth turned up at the corners, and his dark eyes laughed along with mine. "Congrats, you guys. Now, if I could only talk your sister into having another one. We need to keep up with the Joneses—whoops, I mean Donovans."

"We've already discussed that," Gianna said shortly. "I told you, if we do have another child, it won't be for a couple of more years. Maybe once I make partner."

"Are they considering you?" I asked in delight. "That's fantastic!"

She hugged me tightly and then flopped back down on the rug, gathering Alex in her arms. "I think there's a good chance, but we'll have to wait and see."

"Well deserved, *bellissima*," my father said proudly.

Mrs. Gavelli snorted. "Huh. Another baby. What you think of that, Rosa?"

Grandma Rosa raised a glass of wine to her lips and peered over the rim at me. "I think it is wonderful. I have thought it was wonderful for quite a while now."

"No way. You knew?" Mike asked.

My grandmother gave a small shrug. "I was not sure, but I guessed." Her eyes met mine, and she smiled. "And I hoped."

"Hey guys, it's on!" Josie said excitedly.

The opening strands from "Call Me Maybe" filled the room. We watched as a tribute to Smiley flashed across the screen, and there was a moment of silence to honor him. A few seconds later, he was alive again, smiling and waving at the pretend audience as he entered my bakery to tumultuous cheers and clapping.

"I didn't know that you had an audience in the bakery for the taping." My mother sounded insulted. "No one invited us to be there."

"Mom, you were still on your trip," I reminded her.

"Bah." Grandma Rosa frowned. "There was no one there, Maria. It was an artifact audience."

I had to think about this one for a minute. "Do you mean artificial, Grandma?"

She nodded. "I like that too."

"Of course there was no audience," my father boomed. "Nicoletta would have driven them away."

Mrs. Gavelli started to say something in Italian, but Johnny shushed her so that we could hear the introductions being made. At the end of the show, each eligible bachelorette came over to Earl as their full names were announced. He had insisted on kissing Grandma Rosa and Dodie on the cheek, much to their displeasure. The scene with Earl and Nicoletta had been recut after they set eyes on each other, so there was no way for anyone to know he'd passed out.

"Rosa, you pulled that off with a lot of class," Mike commented. "There aren't many people who can conduct themselves with such dignity on a show like that. *Especially* a reality dating show."

"Mike's right," Gianna said. "And think of all the people around the world who were watching. You're famous!"

Grandma Rosa shook her head and made the sign of the cross on her chest. "At least it is all over with."

Mike rose from the couch. "I need a drink. Do you want anything, princess?"

"I'll come with you."

Gianna looked up from the rug and gave me a teasing grin. "Let him wait on you, Sal. Nine months goes by in the blink of an eye."

"That must be why I had four kids," Josie quipped. "For all that extra attention."

Everyone laughed as Mike and I left the room. I desperately wanted another cup of coffee but needed to watch my caffeine intake. Before I could decide, Mike poured a glass of milk and handed it to me.

I made a face. "You know I'm not a big fan."

"The calcium is good for you," he said. "Look at it this way. It's one of the ingredients in cheesecake."

"Well, when you put it that way, how can I refuse?" I took a sip and smacked my lips. "Oh, yum. Delicious."

He chuckled and put his arms around me. "You're not a good liar, Sal. I should have known you were pregnant, even though the test said otherwise. You look beautiful and have the same glow as when you were expecting Cookie."

"It's a glow from happiness."

He placed his mouth over mine and kissed me passionately. When we broke apart, he buried his lips in my hair. "I have everything I could want now. A beautiful wife, an adorable little girl, and another baby on the way. The only thing that would make me happier is if you could manage to stay out of danger. Maybe your grandmother is right."

"What do you mean?"

"I'm talking about the time she said that you were meant to help people in this life," he explained. "You know—when she said it was your density to solve murders."

I laughed out loud. In her usual fashion, Grandma Rosa had managed to mix up her words. "It isn't like I go looking for trouble," I reminded him.

Mike nodded. "Yeah, I understand that these things happen. But I wish they'd happen to someone else. And I want you to promise me that you'll be extra careful during this pregnancy and not take any risks."

"That goes without saying," I said. "This baby means everything to me."

He stroked my cheek tenderly. "Me too. Are you hoping for a boy or girl?"

"A little boy would be nice," I admitted. "I'd like a son to carry on the Donovan name. What about you?"

His midnight-blue eyes gazed into mine with love. "Honestly? I don't care. As long as the baby and you are healthy, that's all that matters to me. Another daughter would be nice. I guess I like being surrounded by beautiful women." Mike paused for a second. "Hey, maybe we'll get lucky and have one of each."

"Twins?" I panicked inwardly at the thought.

Mike grinned. "We better check the fortune cookies and see what they say."

CHAPTER TWENTY-ONE

My father raised his glass. "I'd like to propose a toast to the newest member of the Muccio family. May he or she be as good-looking as their grandfather."

Everyone laughed and raised their glasses. With the exception of my ginger ale and Cookie's and Alex's milk, the rest of my family was drinking champagne. Josie and her brood had plans to watch her oldest son play in a baseball tournament, but she'd sent along some of her delicious champagne cookies to help us celebrate the special occasion.

My father took a bite of one and closed his eyes while he chewed. "That Josie can sure make a mean cookie."

After one sip of champagne, Gianna made a face and poured herself a glass of Chardonnay. "Too bubbly for my taste."

My mother beamed at everyone around the large cherrywood dining table. "This is the best feeling," she sighed happily. "I love having my entire family around me. And at this time next year, there will be one more person at the table."

Mike kissed my cheek as I indulged in another helping of Grandma Rosa's braciole. We'd had such a good time last night that my parents had insisted we all come for Sunday dinner to continue the momentum. "Isn't it funny? Now that I know what's wrong, I don't feel as sick anymore. Maybe it was partially mind over matter."

My father nodded as he spooned tomato sauce over his braciole and a piece of freshly baked Italian bread. "Most likely. Positive thinking is the key to life, baby girl. Take me, for instance. My aura shines through this room like the sun. I mean, how else do you think I stay in such good shape?"

Gianna shook her head and saluted him with her glass of wine. "You're definitely one in a million, Dad."

"I only saw good comments about *Senior Moments* online

today," my mother announced. "Jerry Maroon wrote a nice article, too."

"He must be turning over a new page," Grandma Rosa remarked.

"I think you mean leaf, Grandma."

She nodded gravely. "I like that too."

Mike took the paper plate with pasta that I had cut up into tiny pieces for Cookie and placed it on her highchair tray. "I guess I can't really be mad at him anymore. After all, he did save Sal's life."

Grandma Rosa sat down in the chair next to mine and helped herself to some pasta. "I am not sure how everyone got our landline number, but the phone has been ringing all morning. So many people that I do not even know have called to congratulate me." She twirled her finger in a circular motion next to her short white hair. "They are a bunch of nutsy cookies."

I decided to let that one go.

My phone buzzed for the second time in the last five minutes, but I ignored it. This was quality family time, and Dad disliked interruptions at the table, unless he was causing them.

As I reached for another piece of homemade bread still warm from the oven, my parents' landline rang. Grandma Rosa started to rise, but I held up a hand. "I'll grab it, Grandma. You've done enough. Sit and enjoy your dinner."

To my surprise, she didn't argue. Grandma Rosa seemed somewhat subdued, and I was still concerned about her. I figured she would improve because the trip was back on, but that had not been the case.

With a sigh, I went into the kitchen and grabbed the receiver off the wall. "Hello."

"Sal!" Josie shrieked. "I've been trying to reach you."

I sucked in a breath. "What is it? Are you okay?"

"Don't worry, no one died," she assured me.

Thank goodness for small favors.

Josie continued. "Since the episode of *Senior Moments* aired last night, we've been getting all kinds of messages on our Facebook page, from all over the world! Some have been from nutcases who want to know if they can be on TV too, but most are for orders."

"Wow, that's great! But you figured that would happen, so why all the excitement?" Social media was more of Josie's thing. I rarely checked our Facebook or Instagram pages, leaving it all to her.

"Let me finish." Josie's voice was breathless with excitement. "A little while ago, a message came in that I think you will want to see."

"Well, if it's for an order, let's deal with it tomorrow." I had already decided that once the baby was born, I needed to cut down on my days at the bakery. Josie would be getting a large and well-deserved raise to handle more of the financial matters, while Dodie was fine with working extra hours. It was time to take a step back and focus on my growing family.

"Sal, you have to check this out as soon as possible," Josie continued. "Please go to the messages and have a look, okay? That's all I'm going to say. I don't want to ruin the surprise. The message starts out, 'Attention: Mrs. Sally Donovan.' Gotta run."

My curiosity had piqued. I hung up the receiver and grabbed my cell from the pocket of my shorts. I logged into Facebook and started to check the messages on our page. Josie had been right. There were dozens of orders and a few *Congratulations* messages as well. I found the one that Josie had mentioned and began to read it.

"Oh, my God." My hands started to shake, and all I could do was stare at the message for several seconds, trying to wrap my head around the words. This couldn't be happening. What were the chances?

"Sal, your dinner is getting cold," my mother called.

"Grandma." My voice shook as I went to the doorway between the kitchen and dining room. "Can you come out here for a minute, please?"

Everyone glanced up from the table. "Sal, are you sick?" Mike asked. "You're as pale as a ghost."

"No, I'm fine," I managed to choke out. "But there's something I need to talk to Grandma about."

"It must be the oven again," my mother mused. "We really need a new one, Domenic."

My father clinked his wineglass against hers. "No offense, hot stuff, but the last time that you actually used the oven was…never?"

Everyone laughed as Grandma Rosa pushed back her chair and followed me to the kitchen. When her gaze met mine, she wrinkled her brow. "Are you all right, my dear girl?"

I closed the door behind us and held out my phone. "Grandma, you need to see this message I received."

She shook her head "*Cara mia*, I left my reading glasses upstairs. The print on those phones is too tiny to make out. You read it for me, please."

"Are you sure?" I asked, and she nodded.

My heart was pounding so hard that I was certain she could hear. I tried to remain calm, but it was impossible.

Attention: Mrs. Sally Donovan, Proprietor, Sally's Samples

Good day madam,

I trust that you will be good enough to forward this message to your grandmother, Mrs. Rosa Belgacci.

My dearest Rosa,

I saw you on television last evening. It has been many years, but I would know you anywhere. Those beautiful eyes, windows to your soul, have not changed one bit.

Do you remember when we were courting? I promised that we would always be together, but there were circumstances we could not avoid. When I returned from the Vietnam War several years later after being a POW, you had already left the country. Your parents refused to tell me where you were. I looked for you for a long time and wondered if perhaps our love was not meant to be. But now, I realize that fate has brought us back together.

I am alive and well and living in Sicily. It is my greatest hope that we can meet again soon and see if our love story can continue to the next chapter.

Please write back. I eagerly await your reply.

With love always,

Vernon

The silence in the room was deafening as I looked up. Grandma Rosa stood there, motionless, with her face carved out of stone. She sat down in a chair looking dazed and didn't speak for several seconds.

"How can this be," she whispered. "I thought for certain that he was dead."

My heart was consumed with happiness. "No one can be right all the time, Grandma. Not even you. Vernon sounds very much alive to me. And he wants to see you. What are you going to do?"

My grandmother stared at me in silence, her soulful brown eyes filled with unshed tears. A moment later, her beautiful smile lit up the entire room. "Well, then. Italy, here I come."

RECIPES

Champagne Crème Sandwich Cookies

Ingredients for cookies:
1 box of white cake mix
1 (5.1 ounce) box instant vanilla pudding
2 eggs, room temperature
1/2 cup unsalted butter, melted and slightly cooled
1/4 cup champagne (or substitute prosecco or sparkling wine)
Gold sprinkles and coarse white sparkling sugar

Filling
1 cup unsalted butter, softened
3 cups confectioners' sugar
1/4 teaspoon salt
1 teaspoon vanilla extract
2 - 3 tablespoons champagne (prosecco or sparkling wine)

For the cookies:
Add the cake mix, instant pudding, eggs, melted butter, and champagne to a large bowl. Using an electric mixer, beat until smooth, about 2 minutes. Cover dough with plastic wrap and place in the refrigerator for 1 hour. Preheat the oven to 350 degrees Fahrenheit. Line baking sheets with parchment paper. Roll the cookie dough into equal-sized balls, about 1-1/2 to 2-inches in diameter. Depending on the size of the balls, you should have 36 - 40 cookies.

Combine equal parts of gold sprinkles with the coarse white sparkling sugar (start with 3 tablespoons each) in a shallow, wide bowl, or dinner plate. Add more sprinkles as needed. Press the top

of each cookie dough ball into the sprinkles and place, sprinkle side up, on the parchment-lined baking sheet. Slightly flatten the tops of the cookies.
Bake cookies for 8 - 10 minutes, rotating the cookie sheets halfway through baking. Cookies should be slightly golden brown on the edges. Cool the cookies on the baking sheet for 5 minutes then transfer to a wire rack to cool completely before filling with the buttercream.

For the filling:
Beat the softened butter on medium-high speed for 2 -3 minutes until creamy. Turn the mixer to low and add the confectioners' sugar, half a cup at a time, beating well after each addition. Add in the vanilla, salt, and 2 tablespoons champagne. Beat on medium-high for 5 minutes, until light and fluffy. If buttercream appears too thick, add in additional champagne, 1 teaspoon at a time, until desired consistency is reached. Place the filling into a pastry bag fitted with a large star tip. Match up two cookies, according to equal sizes as best as possible. Pipe swirls of buttercream on the bottom of one cookie. Gently press the second cookie (bottom side facing the buttercream) into the filling. Repeat with remaining cookie pairs. Makes approximately 18 - 20 sandwich cookies.

Cherry Almond Cookies

1 cup butter, softened
1 cup brown sugar
2 cups all-purpose flour
½ cup sliced blanched almonds
½ cup chopped red candied cherries
2 ounces white chocolate (Optional)

Preheat oven to 350 degrees Fahrenheit. Line bottom and sides of an 11x7-inch glass baking pan with parchment paper; leave paper hanging over pan edges so that cookies can be lifted out after baking.

Beat butter and brown sugar together with an electric mixer until light and fluffy, about 2 minutes. Stir flour into butter mixture until crumbly; stir in almonds and cherries. Press mixture evenly into the bottom of prepared pan. Bake in the preheated oven until lightly golden at edges, about 20 minutes. Score with a sharp knife into bars while in the pan and still warm; allow cookies to cool about 30 minutes. Lift cookies from pan and slice to separate along scored marks.

Melt white chocolate in a microwave-safe glass or ceramic bowl in 30-second intervals, stirring after each melting, for 1 to 3 minutes depending on your microwave. Do not overheat or chocolate will scorch. Drizzle melted white chocolate over cookies or dip half of each cookie into melted white chocolate.

Fudgy Cosmic Brownie Cookies

½ cup unsalted butter softened
½ cup light brown sugar
¼ cup granulated sugar
1 large egg
1 teaspoon vanilla extract
2 tablespoons light corn syrup (not the same as high fructose corn syrup)
¼ teaspoon baking soda
¼ teaspoon salt
½ cup dark cocoa powder (Hershey's Special Dark is recommended)
1¼ cup all-purpose flour

Toppings:
¾ cup semi-sweet chocolate chips
¼ cup heavy cream
Rainbow chip sprinkles

Preheat oven to 350 degrees Fahrenheit. In a large bowl, use an electric mixer on medium-high speed to cream softened unsalted butter (½ cup, 1 stick), light brown sugar (½ cup), and granulated sugar (¼ cup) for 2 minutes until light and fluffy. Add the egg (1 large), vanilla extract (1 teaspoon), and light corn syrup (2 tablespoons) and mix on low speed until combined. Scrape down the sides of the bowl so everything can combine. Add in baking soda (¼ teaspoon) and salt (¼ teaspoon) and mix for another 5-10 seconds until combined. Lastly, add dark cocoa powder (½ cup) and all-purpose flour (1 ¼ cups) and mix on medium until combined.
Scoop dough into 1/4 cup (4 tablespoons) sized scoops roll into balls, then gently flatten each dough ball into a 1/2" thick disc; this will help them spread instead of being puffy.
Bake at 350°F for 11-12 minutes. Do not overbake. The centers may look a tiny bit wet but will continue to bake on the hot pan, allowing them to firm up without overbaking.
Allow to fully cool before decorating.
To Make Chocolate Ganache:

In a medium-sized, heat-safe bowl (cereal bowl sized), place semi-sweet chocolate chips (¾ cup).

In a separate medium-sized bowl or large liquid measuring cup, heat heavy cream (¼ cup) in the microwave for 30-45 seconds, or until it begins to bubble (it's important that your measuring cup or bowl is at least 4x taller than the milk line, as it will expand when it's heating and can easily overflow). You can also heat this on the stove; remove it once it begins to steam.

Use a hot pad to carefully remove milk from the microwave and pour over the chocolate chips (do not stir yet!). Use a fork to press down the chips so that they're fully covered with the cream.

Allow to sit for about 3 minutes, then use a fork to stir; it will be thick and will likely look like it's not going to mix together but keep at it until smooth & creamy.
If your mixture doesn't melt down, microwave in 10 second increments at 50% power, stirring in between each increment until smooth.
To decorate: Spoon 1 tablespoon of chocolate ganache on each cookie and top with rainbow chip sprinkles. Place in refrigerator for 30-60 minutes to help the ganache harden. If you refrigerate the cookies, they become even fudgier when chilled! You can also keep them at room temperature for up to 2 days, if desired.

Makes 8 large cookies.

Easy Sugar Cookies

2 3/4 cups all-purpose flour
1 teaspoon baking soda
3/4 teaspoon salt
1/2 teaspoon baking powder
1 cup unsalted butter, at cool room temperature
1 3/4 cups of granulated sugar
1 large egg plus 1 large egg yolk
1 tablespoon pure vanilla extract
1/2 cup granulated sugar, for rolling cookies in

Preheat oven to 350 degrees Fahrenheit. Line a large baking sheet with parchment paper and set aside. In a medium bowl, whisk together the flour, baking soda, salt, and baking powder. Set aside. In the bowl of a stand mixer fitted with the paddle attachment, beat the butter on medium speed for 1 minute. Add the granulated sugar (1 ¾ cups) and beat until light and fluffy, about 2 to 3 minutes. I always stop once and scrape down the sides of the bowl with a spatula and continue mixing. Add the egg, egg yolk, vanilla extract and mix until well combined.

Add the dry ingredients and mix on low until just combined. The dough might look a little crumbly at first, but it will come together and be just fine. Put the remaining sugar in a small bowl. Form the dough into balls, about 2 tablespoons per cookie. Roll each ball in the sugar until well coated. Place on the prepared baking sheet, about 2-inches apart.
Bake for 10 to 14 minutes or until the bottoms are light golden brown and the cookies start to crack. Don't over bake or the cookies won't be soft and chewy. Remove the pan from the oven and let the cookies cool on the baking sheet for 5 minutes. Transfer the cookies to a cooling rack and cool completely.

Makes about two dozen cookies.

ABOUT THE AUTHOR

USA Today bestselling author Catherine Bruns lives in Upstate New York with a male dominated household that consists of her very patient husband, three sons, and assorted cats and dogs. She has wanted to be a writer since the age of eight when she wrote her own version of Cinderella (fortunately Disney never sued). Catherine holds a B.A. in English and is a member of Mystery Writers of America and Sisters in Crime.

To learn more about Catherine Bruns, visit her online at:
www.catherinebruns.net

Enjoyed this book? Check out these Aloha Lagoon Mysteries by Catherine Bruns!

Made in United States
Troutdale, OR
07/21/2024

21435923R00119